THE SHRINE

A DCI RYAN MYSTERY

LJ Ross

OTHER BOOKS BY LJ ROSS

The Alexander Gregory Thrillers in order:

1. Impostor

2. Hysteria

3. Bedlam

The DCI Ryan Mysteries in order:

1. Holy Island

2. Sycamore Gap

3. Heavenfield

4. Angel

5. High Force

6. Cragside

7. Dark Skies

8. Seven Bridges

9. The Hermitage

10. Longstone

11. The Infirmary (prequel)

12. The Moor

13. Penshaw

14. Borderlands

15. Ryan's Christmas

16. The Shrine

"Even the darkest night will end, and the sun will rise."

—Victor Hugo, *Les Misérables*

CHAPTER 1

I t was a perfect spring day.

Sunshine bathed the city of Durham in golden light, warming the ancient stone walls of the castle and neighbouring university, where students spilled out of its panelled hallways to sprawl over the grassy quadrangle known as Palace Green. They wore carefully mismatched, overpriced garments designed to resemble working class attire from a bygone era, and the lawn became a patchwork of muted beige and stone-washed denim. Far above, the cathedral loomed, its Gothic walls rising up over two hundred feet to dominate the landscape for as far as the eye could see, casting long shadows over the people who scurried like ants far below.

Doctor Anna Taylor-Ryan joined their number and settled herself upon one of the shady wooden benches overlooking the Green. She was in the process of unwrapping a sandwich when a tiny foot connected sharply with her bladder.

"*Hey!*" she said, tapping her swollen belly. "What d'you think you're doing in there—playing football?"

There came another swift jab in reply.

"You definitely get this from your father's side," she muttered.

Abandoning all thoughts of picnicking in the sunshine, she grabbed her bag and cast an urgent glance around the vicinity for the nearest bathroom. To her left, the north door to the cathedral was open to the public, beckoning them inside to discover a thousand years of history.

And, more importantly, its cloakroom facilities.

"C'mon," she said, choosing to include her unborn baby in the conversation she carried on with herself. "Let's make a run for it."

She made a hasty beeline across the grass, half-walking, half-waddling towards an enormous, carved wooden door featuring a bronze replica of the infamous 'Sanctuary Knocker', which had once admitted twelfth-century fugitives into the cathedral's protective fold.

Though she was no fugitive, Anna hurried inside with all speed, barely noticing the ornamental columns and circular arches of the nave, nor the spectacular stained-glass window at its eastern end, designed in the shape of a rose.

"Excuse me," she puffed at one of the volunteers. "Can you tell me where the nearest ladies' room is?"

The young man wore a blue t-shirt bearing an embroidered logo in the shape of Saint Cuthbert's pectoral cross, a priceless artefact kept on display in one of the exhibition rooms.

"There are some in the Open Treasure Galleries," he said, pointing towards the entrance to the exhibition rooms. "You go through there and follow the signs—it's a one-way system."

Anna thanked him, but her spirits fell when she saw the line of tourists queueing to enter.

"Bugger," she said, drawing a disapproving glance from an elderly couple passing by.

And balls, she added silently. If she didn't find a bathroom soon, a lot more than bad language was going to sully the House of God, and then they'd *really* have something to worry about.

With a sudden flash of inspiration, she remembered there was a cloakroom near the exhibition exit, which was located through the cloister a short way off.

With single-minded determination, Anna bypassed the queue, hustling past tour groups, students she half-recognised and bemused members of the public until she reached the back entrance to the Open Treasure Galleries.

"Excuse me, miss—excuse me! You can't come in this way…you're supposed to go around the other way!"

"This is an emergency!"

Anna barged past the steward on the door, who made a half-hearted attempt to follow her until the nature of her emergency became clear.

"That was a close call," she told the baby, when they re-emerged a few minutes later into an area of the cathedral called the Great Kitchen. It had been repurposed since the days when it was used to feed hungry clerics, and was now a state-of-the-art exhibition space, featuring several priceless artefacts belonging to the region's most famous saint, Cuthbert.

She had viewed the collection many times before, but Anna never grew tired of studying clues to the past and soon found herself mesmerised by the gleaming golden lines of Cuthbert's cross, displayed behind a thick wall of glass.

A sudden movement in her peripheral vision broke the spell and she started to turn.

Danger, a voice whispered. *There's danger, here.*

But she was not quick enough.

Seconds later, there came a series of deafening explosions and she fell to her knees, throwing her arms around her belly to protect the baby.

Smoke filled the room quickly—thick and pungent—and she struggled to her feet, coughing and clutching her stomach as she stumbled towards the exit. Wailing cries of terror filtered through the ringing in her ears and, beneath it, there came the sound of a heavy thud followed by a crash somewhere over her left shoulder.

Terrified now, Anna reached out a hand to feel her way forward, blinking rapidly, eyes streaming while her chest heaved and her mind raced.

Which way?

Which way out?

The blow came from behind, hard and fast, and she tumbled to the floor.

Before darkness fell, her last thoughts were of the man she loved and the baby she carried.

* * *

As fire engines and other emergency services raced through winding, cobbled streets towards Durham Cathedral, Detective Chief Inspector Joan Tebbutt made herself a cup of builder's tea in the small galley kitchen of her home in the town of Seaham, a short drive to the east. Rod Stewart crooned on the radio and dappled sunlight streamed through the window, illuminating a half-completed crossword and plate of custard creams still waiting to be dunked.

When the phone began to shrill, she sighed.

It was her day off and, barring major emergencies, every man and woman in her team knew that she was not to be disturbed on her day off.

She'd already spoken to her daughter and so, aside from a salesman trying to flog insurance she didn't need, that left only one possibility.

Major emergency.

She answered on the third ring.

"Tebbutt."

"Sorry to disturb you at home, ma'am—"

She cut across her sergeant, who sounded nervous. "What's happened?"

"We've had several reports of an incident in progress at Durham Cathedral."

A second's pause, while her heart fell. "What kind of incident?"

"Terror-related. Less than five minutes ago, we received reports of a major explosion. The Fire Service are responding, and Control Room have dispatched first responders to the scene—"

Tebbutt thought quickly.

"Contact Counter-Terrorism," she ordered. "Get on to the bomb squad—it'll be quickest to put a direct call in to the Explosives Ordnance Disposal Unit based out of Otterburn."

She warred with herself, then came to a decision.

"And, Carter? Get on the blower to Ryan, over at Northumbria. Tell him…look, just ask him to get in touch. It's important."

She ended the call and hurried into the hallway, pausing only to grab a jacket and scoop up her keys and warrant card.

She'd need her protective vest, but that was in the boot of her car.

"Right," she muttered, and flung open the front door.

She heard the motorbike before she saw it and, when she did, there was no time to react. The first shot penetrated the side of her neck and, as the pathologist would later remark, she might have survived that.

But the second…

The second hit its mark and she died where she fell, her body kept warm by the early afternoon sunshine.

CHAPTER 2

Northumbria Police Headquarters
Newcastle upon Tyne

D etective Chief Inspector Maxwell Finley-Ryan paused outside the main entrance to Northumbria Police Headquarters and tipped his face up to the sky. He closed his eyes for a moment and smiled—a rare thing, for a man in his line of work. It transformed the angles of his face, so that he was no longer a tall, distant man who'd seen more death than he'd like to remember, but somebody else—somebody younger, who still saw beauty in the world.

And, why not? he thought.

For the first time in years, the number of violent deaths had reduced in their region, thanks to the efforts of Operation Watchman, a cross-constabulary initiative designed to combat a new wave of organised crime in the North East, which he'd been tasked to lead. The trade in illegal drugs had moved along 'County Lines', spreading its poison beyond city limits and established supply chains, trailing violence in its wake. Only by working together and sharing resources had they been able to root out systemic corruption in Northumbria, Durham and Cleveland— and disband one of the worst crime syndicates in living memory. There was still more work to do and, wherever weeds were pulled, more would surely grow, but it was progress worth smiling about.

If things were on an even keel at work, life at home was positively blissful.

For all the tragedies he'd known, Ryan considered himself a lucky man and never more so than the day he'd found Anna—the other, better half of himself. To his unending surprise, she continued to love him despite all the long hours at work, the inherent risks involved in fulfilling his duty to the public and the shadows which followed him, long after he'd clocked out of the office. In light of that, he'd taken it upon himself to make some adjustments, especially now that there would soon be another face to fall in love with.

Ryan's smile widened, and he wondered again whether the baby was a boy or a girl.

It didn't matter, so long as mother and baby were both healthy and happy.

His eyes snapped open as a cloud passed over the sun, shivering when the air turned suddenly cold. All the new parenting books he'd read over the past few months had told him it was normal for expectant fathers to worry, and he was no exception. He worried about the kind of father he would make, about whether he would become a carbon copy of his own—distant, emotionally absent but ultimately well-meaning—or something else? Something better, and of his own creation?

Ryan hoped it would be the latter.

Most of all, he worried about Anna, and wished he could do something more to ease the burden she carried. Foot rubs, scented baths and cuddles were in unlimited supply, but he could not bring their baby into the world, much as he wished he could. He could only marvel at the miracle of it all and wonder how women had ever come to be known as the 'weaker' sex.

He shook his head in disbelief.

Just then, the mobile phone he kept in the back pocket of his jeans began to ring, and he balanced a tray of takeaway coffee carefully in the palm of one hand so he could make a grab for it with the other. He'd barely grasped it when he spotted Detective Constable Melanie Yates running across the entrance foyer, waving her hand wildly to signal him over.

"Morrison wants to see you in her office—she said it was urgent!"

Ryan looked down at the phone he still held in his hand, which had stopped ringing. The caller had been a number he didn't recognise, and he gave a light shrug.

If it was important, they'd leave a message.

"I'm on my way," he said.

* * *

Ryan passed the coffee tray into Yates' capable hands, then took the stairs two at a time until he reached the Executive Suite, where he was ushered into the Chief Constable's office without delay. He found Sandra Morrison seated at her desk, a telephone receiver in one hand and a biro in the other, which she used to scrawl rapid notes. She looked up briefly as he entered the room and Ryan stood to attention, unconsciously adopting the straight-backed, military posture he'd learned from his father.

Morrison ended the call and ran agitated hands through her short blonde hair, tucking it behind her ears. That, more than anything else, gave him cause for concern; she was not a woman given to overtly feminine gestures, except in moments of disquiet.

"Thanks for coming so quickly."

"You said it was urgent, ma'am."

"It is."

She gestured towards one of the visitors' chairs arranged in front of her desk.

"I won't beat around the bush," she said. "There's been a major incident in Durham."

Durham…where Anna worked.

Ryan glanced at the clock on the wall, which read half-past-twelve. He'd checked the news before heading out to buy coffee for his team, and there'd been nothing unusual to report.

But, as he knew only too well, things could change in the blink of an eye.

"There's been a terror explosion at the cathedral," Morrison continued.

"How bad?"

"Too early to say. They're evacuating the immediate area, but they can't go inside the cathedral to assess the damage before the bomb squad have cleared it—"

"What about the university?" Ryan interrupted her, while his mouth ran dry and his palms began to sweat. His wife worked in the History Faculty, which was only a stone's throw from the cathedral.

Morrison cleared her throat.

"I've received no reports of any related incidents at the university," she said. "My understanding is that the explosion was isolated, but nearby buildings are being evacuated as a precaution."

Good, Ryan thought. *That was good.*

But his fingers itched to call Anna, to be sure.

"The situation is an evolving one, but the terror explosion isn't my main concern at present."

He wondered what could possibly be worse than the desecration of a UNESCO World Heritage Site, not to mention the human cost, as yet untold.

"You remember Joan Tebbutt?"

He nodded slowly.

DCI Tebbutt was a colleague in the neighbouring constabulary at Durham CID—a fair-minded woman in her late fifties, who'd been drafted in to investigate the death of their former superintendent a couple of years prior. She'd done a thorough, unbiased job, and he'd respected her enormously for it.

Ryan braced himself.

"She was killed, less than fifteen minutes ago," Morrison said quietly.

There was a moment's silence before training kicked in.

"How did it happen?"

"On her doorstep, at home," she said, grateful for the shop talk. "Neighbours reported shots fired, and first responders attended the scene. There was a squad car nearby—probably on its way to the city centre—and they recognised Joan immediately."

Ryan thought of the timing.

"It can't be coincidence that this happened within minutes of the cathedral going up."

"Possibly not...on the other hand, Joan was responsible for cleaning up Durham CID after Operation Watchman, not counting all the other cases she's closed over the years. She was an outstanding detective with a proven track record, which made her a target."

Ryan felt an odd, rippling sensation in his belly, as though someone had stepped on his own grave. If Tebbutt had been a target despite keeping a low profile, he knew the same could equally be said of himself.

It was an unsettling thought.

"Major Crimes in Durham are stretched to breaking point," Morrison continued. "Watchman cleaned out half of their senior staff, and they haven't had time to recruit anybody to replace them. Tebbutt would have been the natural choice to lead on the terror incident at the cathedral."

"Who's stepped in?"

"Temporarily, her sergeant—Ben Carter. A safe pair of hands, so I'm told."

Ryan nodded, understanding the task which lay ahead. Only a detective of sufficient rank and independence could be entrusted to investigate Tebbutt's death, which ruled out Sergeant Carter or anybody else in Durham CID.

"You need me to take over," he surmised.

Morrison nodded.

"This couldn't have come at a worse moment," she said. "Tebbutt was the linchpin holding things together in the Durham office."

"Joan was one of our own," Ryan said quietly. "She deserves the best."

Morrison smiled for the first time.

"That's why you're sitting here now," she said. "Fact is, Ryan, you're just about the only person around these parts who's had the misfortune to have seen it all before."

"Not quite the *only* person."

Ryan thought of his team of detectives, who'd seen plenty in their time and could be trusted in any emergency.

"Take whoever you need," she said. "Leave us with a skeleton staff here—we can manage, in the meantime."

"Thank you, ma'am."

No more words were necessary and Ryan rose to his feet, preparing to leave.

"Tebbutt was a good detective," Morrison said, softly. "She didn't deserve to die that way."

"Nobody does," he replied. "When I find whoever did this, there'll be a reckoning."

There was ice in his voice but there was also conviction, and Morrison released the long breath she'd been holding since her telephone had rung twenty minutes before. If anyone could clean up this almighty mess, he could.

"Be careful," she said.

He gave a brief nod, and then was gone.

* * *

The moment Ryan stepped back into the wide, functional corridor outside Morrison's office, he retrieved the mobile phone from his pocket. Ordering himself to remain calm, he fumbled with the speed dial until Anna's number began to ring.

No answer.

He pressed redial, uncaring of who was forced to step around him as he lingered in the passageway.

"Come on," he muttered. "Pick up."

But there was still no answer.

CHAPTER 3

In an open-plan office on the floor below, Detective Sergeant Frank Phillips leaned back in his chair, sank his teeth into a fresh ham-and-pease-pudding stottie, and let out a *purring* sound of satisfaction. A man of his years and experience could boast of having tried most things, but few could compare with the untold joy of a freshly baked roll on a sunny afternoon.

"That's better than sex," he mumbled.

"I beg your pardon?"

Detective Inspector Denise MacKenzie—his wife and, incidentally, his senior in the police hierarchy—cocked her head around the side of her computer monitor and gave him the Death Stare, causing him to choke on the remaining crumbs.

"I didn't mean…" He coughed loudly, and rapped a fist against his chest. "It was just a figure of speech—"

"If I thought for one minute that our love life was being compared with a *ham sandwich*, so help me, Frank Phillips—"

He considered the merits of entering into a debate about why a stottie was far superior to the average ham sandwich, then thought better of it.

"Nothing in the world can compare with you, my love," he said, with a toothy smile.

MacKenzie let out a disbelieving snort, but any further comment was forestalled by the persistent ringing of Ryan's desk phone.

Phillips leaned over to snatch it up.

"Major Crimes," he said, breezily. "No, sorry, he's not at his desk at the moment. This is DS Phillips, if you want to leave a message—"

Within seconds, his tone changed.

"You're sure? Right…yes, alright, I'll let him know. We'll get there as quickly as we can."

Phillips replaced the receiver.

"Frank? What's the matter?"

But there was no time to answer before Ryan entered the room, long legs eating up the floor as he made directly for his coat and car keys. Phillips swallowed the tight ball of emotion lodged in his throat, and came to his feet.

"Ryan—" he began.

"Not now," his friend muttered. "I need to get hold of Anna—there's been a terror attack in Durham, and she's not answering her phone—"

Phillips closed his eyes briefly, then opened them again.

"Aye, lad, I know."

Ryan turned slowly to look at him.

"How…how do *you* know, Frank?"

Phillips glanced around the room at their colleagues, who were doing an admirable job of staring at their computer screens in an attempt to give them some privacy.

"Howay, let's step outside—"

"What is it, Frank? What's happened?"

Ryan's voice trembled, but he preferred to hear the truth, no matter how ugly, nor how hard.

Phillips gave it to him.

"It's Anna," he said. "They found her inside the cathedral…she's badly hurt, son."

All colour drained from Ryan's face. He felt numb, weightless, and black spots began to dance in front of his eyes.

"Is she still alive?" he whispered.

Phillips nodded.

"She was taken to Durham University Hospital, but they're transferring her to the Intensive Care Unit at the RVI," he said, referring to the larger hospital in Newcastle.

"The baby," Ryan said, almost inaudibly. "Is it…Frank—?"

His eyes were no longer a clear grey, but dark, swirling pools of misery in his ashen face.

"I don't know," Phillips said, honestly.

There was a stillness in the room, as though time had been suspended. The men and women of the Major Crimes Unit watched with compassion as their leader drew himself up to his full height, and tried to arrange his features into a professional mask.

"Yates, Lowerson? Report to the Chief Constable," Ryan said, tremulously. "There's been a major incident, and you're needed on duty. Morrison will bring you up to speed."

They looked between themselves, then nodded dumbly.

"The rest of you—" he began, and then trailed off, not quite able to find the words.

MacKenzie stepped forward and placed a gentle hand on Ryan's back, feeling the muscles jump beneath her touch.

"We'll be with you," she said. "Whatever happens, we'll be right there beside you."

* * *

MacKenzie drove the short distance from Police Headquarters to the Royal Victoria Infirmary. Her hands were capable and confident on the wheel and, when they encountered light traffic on the main road leading into the city centre, she didn't hesitate to activate the siren on her car, knowing there wouldn't be a police officer in the constabulary who'd dare to argue that theirs wasn't an emergency.

Ryan said not a word throughout the journey, turning his face away to stare unseeingly out of the passenger window. But, as they entered the hospital car park, he spoke again.

"What will I do, if I lose her?"

MacKenzie turned off the engine, wishing she knew what to say and how to say it. Though she had spoken to the victims of crime and their families many times before, there was no manual she could turn to when the pain was so close to home. Ryan and Anna were her closest friends and the possibility of losing one, or both of them, was unimaginable.

"Don't think like that," she said, firmly. "Anna is still alive and that's all that matters. Isn't that right, Frank?"

"Aye, that's right," Phillips said, leaning forward to put a steadying hand on Ryan's shoulder. "Keep the faith, lad."

Ryan almost laughed at the choice of words. He'd never believed in a higher power; not when his sister was murdered, nor any time he'd looked upon the wasted bodies of the dead.

But now…

Now, he'd worship the moon and the stars, if only they'd let Anna stay with him a little longer.

* * *

Ryan's footsteps echoed around the long corridors of the Royal Victoria Infirmary like a death knell. He knew the way to the Critical Care Unit on Ward 18—he'd walked this road many times before, but never as a husband or an expectant father. He was flanked on either side by Phillips and MacKenzie and, though his mind did not recognise it at the time, he would later know that their silent presence was part of the reason he was able to put one foot in front of the other.

They were buzzed inside by one of the Ward Managers, who directed them into a private consulting room. It was a small, windowless space painted in a drab shade of off-white, but somebody had obviously tried to cheer it up with the addition of some generic art prints on the walls and a large, artificial plant. Four sagging chairs had been arranged around a central coffee table, in the middle of which was an empty box of tissues and several stacks of leaflets and business cards ranging from grief counselling to physiotherapy.

To their eyes, it looked exactly like the family room back at Police Headquarters, a space only ever used to convey bad news. Ryan felt a surge of irrational anger, and his hands curled into fists by his sides.

"Why have they brought me in here?" he snarled, at nobody in particular. "I want to see Anna—"

"Mr Ryan?"

The door opened to admit one of the consultant neurologists, who wore a neutral, unreadable expression and a badge which read, 'MR RICHARD BARKER'.

Ryan stepped forward.

"Yes. Yes, I'm here for my wife, Anna—"

"I'm Mr Barker," the consultant said. "Please, take a seat."

He gestured to one of the tired looking chairs, which Ryan ignored.

"How is she?"

There were two types of person, Barker thought. Those who needed a soft approach, and those who preferred unvarnished facts, delivered without preamble. He considered the man standing before him, and gave a brief nod.

"Your wife was admitted around ten minutes ago," he said. "I'm sorry to tell you she's suffered a serious head trauma, which has resulted in bleeding on her brain that requires stemming. We're prepping her for surgery at the moment, so I'm afraid I don't have very long."

MacKenzie reached out a hand to Phillips, who held it tightly in his own.

"How bad is it?" Ryan asked.

"We won't know the true extent until we operate, but I must tell you her situation is complicated by several factors. The most important is that your wife was unconscious when she was discovered, and hasn't yet regained consciousness. That makes it very difficult when performing neurosurgery because, as far as possible, we prefer patients to remain awake so we can be sure their other functions aren't being impaired. However, we have no choice in this case."

Ryan bore down hard, and nodded.

"What about the baby?"

"The baby is still alive," the consultant said, and checked the time on the wall. "We're continuing to monitor her status."

Ryan let out a harsh sob of relief and rubbed a shaking hand over his face, holding back tears by strength of character alone.

Then, slowly, his hand fell away and he raised shining eyes the colour of the sea.

"*Her?*"

Barker looked surprised, then embarrassed.

"What's that?"

"You said, 'her' status."

"Ah, I'm sorry, I may have ruined the surprise—"

"No, don't be sorry," Ryan murmured. "Please, look after them…look after my girls."

The consultant nodded, but his tone remained sombre.

"In addition to the head trauma, your wife has several broken bones in her right arm and ankle. She's also suffering from moderately severe smoke inhalation. Mr Ryan, following her surgery, we may need to induce your wife into a temporary coma, to give her body the time it needs to recover. That means you won't be able to talk to her, so you should prepare yourself for that."

Ryan looked him squarely in the eye.

"What's your prognosis?"

The surgeon didn't answer directly.

"The bleed is a major one, and I need to prep myself for theatre now. The quicker we act, the better her chances. I'll have more information for you after we've operated."

Ryan signed the necessary forms and watched the man leave, before turning back to his friends. Though they tried to conceal it, he saw his own fear reflected in their eyes and he looked away, unable to stand it.

Across the room, his eye fell on a collection of children's books and toys stacked in a small canvas box.

"A little girl," he said, softly. "I'll have to look out my shotgun, won't I, Frank?"

Without a word, Phillips crossed the room to envelop his friend in a hard hug. A moment later, MacKenzie joined them and wrapped her arms tightly around them both.

Only then did the tears come.

CHAPTER 4

Outside, the world continued to turn and the sun continued to shine, while Joan Tebbutt's body grew stiff beneath its glare. Acutely conscious of that fact, Lowerson and Yates made their way to Seaham with all speed.

"It seems wrong for it to be such a beautiful day," Melanie said, as they motored south. "It should be overcast or raining."

The afternoon temperature had peaked in the mid-twenties, which was unseasonably warm for springtime in the north of England and incongruous given their present mood.

"I know what you mean," Lowerson said, turning the air con up another notch. "I can't imagine what Ryan's going through. To lose his sister that way, and now this…"

They fell silent, both imagining the worst, and what that could mean for a man they both admired.

A man they both *loved*.

"The best thing we can do is our jobs," Yates decided. "Ryan's trusting us to take care of the crime scene, so that's what we'll do."

Lowerson nodded.

"It's all we can do."

They made their way through Sunderland and then followed a picturesque B-road running parallel to the coast, until they reached Seaham. To the east, the sea stretched out into the far horizon, where oil tankers moved like snails against a pale blue sky.

"I don't know this area very well," Yates said, as they drove along the promenade. "How about you?"

"My grandparents lived not far from here, so we used to visit sometimes—good fish and chips, around here."

She flashed a smile.

"It used to be very different," he continued. "The harbour used to transport tonnes of coal until things changed for good in the 1980s. Mine closures hit the area pretty hard."

Yates saw an upmarket seaside town with pretty cottages, coffee shops and boutiques, and could see there had been major reinvestment in recent times.

"It's lovely…I bet we couldn't afford to live here."

"We couldn't—I already checked."

Her head whipped around. "You did?"

Lowerson smiled to himself. "Well, you know, I've been thinking—"

"Oh, dear."

"I've been *thinking*, it seems silly, the pair of us spending almost every night together but paying for two separate flats."

He paused to judge her reaction.

"Go on."

"Right. Well, I was wondering…maybe, we could think about…"

"Yes?"

"I'd like to live with you, Mel. All the time," he added, for the avoidance of doubt.

She opened her mouth, but he rushed on.

"I know you've only recently bought your flat," he said. "And, I wouldn't want you to lose your independence—"

"So, what do you suggest?"

"Well, I could sell my flat and use the money to buy somewhere a bit bigger for both of us," he said. "You could rent your place out? Or, if that's no good, I could move in with you and sell or rent out my place. Whatever you prefer."

She understood why he hadn't suggested they use his flat as their base. Though it had been a labour of love for him to renovate, too much had happened there in the last few years for it to remain a happy home.

"Maybe—" she began.

Lowerson told himself not to be downcast. It was too soon, and he was rushing things.

"It's okay," he said, injecting a false note of cheer into his voice. "It was just a daft idea."

Melanie shook her head, wondering if she'd ever be allowed to get a word in edgeways.

"I was going to say, *maybe* there's another option," she told him. "We could pool our resources and buy somewhere together, so it would be yours and mine."

He looked across at her in surprise and delight.

"You'd trust me that much?" he said. "I know our first year together was hard, and I wouldn't blame you, if you wanted to take things slowly. I don't want you to feel pressured into making a quick decision. I just know that I'm happy with you, and I don't want to be with anybody else."

His simple words were all the reassurance she needed. All of life involved some risk, and loving someone was the greatest risk of all, but she didn't want to regret not grasping the opportunity for happiness when it came along.

"So long as you leave most of the decorating decisions to me, I think we'll get along just fine."

The smile he gave her was blinding.

"Can I have an X-Box?"

"Not if you ever want to see me naked."

"Fair enough. What about a cat?"

She knew how much he missed the little cat he used to have.

"Yes," she said tenderly. "We can have a cat."

CHAPTER 5

J oan Tebbutt had been a modest woman.

The ex-miner's cottage where she'd lived was a basic two-up, two-down affair, and had been immaculately kept. That much was obvious even from the outside, where daffodils bloomed in a box on the window ledge and lined the pathway leading to her front door, which was marred only by the forensics tent that now rippled on the afternoon breeze.

In light of the extraordinary circumstances, Chief Constable Morrison had given her approval for Lowerson and Yates to manage the crime scene and supervise the transfer of Tebbutt's body to the mortuary in their temporary role as 'Acting SIOs', until such time as Ryan or another senior detective was able to take over. Though it was good experience, for his part, Lowerson did not relish the responsibility; not merely because it was unpleasant or that it required him to step—albeit briefly—into Ryan's shoes, but because of the unique history he'd shared with the dead woman.

Once, during a brief, unhappy time in his life, Jack Lowerson had found himself in the frame for the murder of their former superintendent—a woman he'd been romantically involved with, much to his regret. Protocol had demanded an independent investigation by a detective outside of his constabulary, and Joan Tebbutt had been the woman for the job. Though he'd suffered Post Traumatic Stress Disorder for a while after, and large portions of his memory were still missing from those days, one thing he could recall was Tebbutt's professionalism and respect for the law.

Clearing his name would have been meaningless if it had not been achieved through the proper process, and he would always be grateful to her for that. Now that the situation was reversed, he carried the burden of ensuring her murder was treated with the same level of respect she'd afforded him, and it weighed heavily on his shoulders. Lowerson doubted he would have been allowed to be a part of the investigation at all, were it not for the fact they were severely understaffed and unlikely to find a detective in the whole of the North East who could swear they didn't have some level of conscious or unconscious bias in finding Tebbutt's killer.

"Morrison said the local police had secured the scene but not entered the property, or moved the body," he said, as they slammed out of the car. "She gave the CSIs the go-ahead to make a start, considering Tebbutt's body has been open to the elements."

"Not to mention, prying eyes," Yates replied, and nodded towards a small crowd that was gathering beside the police cordon. "It happens every time. Why don't they just watch daytime telly to get their jollies, rather than picking over the bones of other people's misfortune?"

"Human nature," he replied.

Pointedly ignoring the men and women who jostled for position to get a better view of the goings-on, they made their way over to where two constables lounged inside a squad car, with their windows down and the radio on.

"You've got to be kidding," Yates muttered. "What the hell do they think this is?"

She slapped her palm against the top of the vehicle.

"Move your arse!" she snapped, pressing her warrant card to the window screen.

There followed a desperate scramble out of the car.

"Sorry, ma'am, we were just taking a—a call on the radio—"

"Don't insult my intelligence," she said. "Why the hell aren't you manning the crime scene?"

"We—we can see it from here," one of them argued.

Yates made a show of turning a full circle, and had her worst suspicions confirmed.

"You can't even see the front door, which means anybody could wander inside. Where's the log, recording entries and exits?" she demanded.

They produced a clipboard.

"The CSIs are already on site, but there's no entry here," she said, furiously, and thrust the clipboard back at them. "First, I want your names, badge numbers and a full report. Then, I want you to plant yourselves over there, where you should have been in the first place."

Lowerson waited patiently while she put the fear of God into the two young constables, and had to admit she was a fine sight when she was all riled up.

His next thought was to wonder, briefly, what she'd be like if he ever left the toilet seat up.

Some things didn't bear thinking about.

* * *

Ryan was thinking of Anna, and of the first time they'd met, five years ago.

It had been Christmas on Lindisfarne—a tiny, atmospheric island separated from mainland Northumberland twice a day by a tidal causeway. It was famous the world over as a place of healing and pilgrimage, where Saint Cuthbert had once lived in the priory and communed with his God, over a thousand years before. Though Ryan couldn't bring himself to believe, he could appreciate the healing properties of seclusion, of peace and quiet away from the rest of the world, and had travelled there to grieve his sister's death in private.

He'd never expected to be called upon to solve a murder, nor to meet the woman he'd want to share his life with.

Anna had changed all that.

The first time he'd seen her standing there, bundled up against the winter chill, he'd recognised a kindred spirit. There was nobody else with whom he'd want to share the everyday joys and heartaches of life, and the prospect of another forty-something years without her beside him was bleak. She was his greatest teacher; patient, honest and wise, and one of the few people in the world able to make him laugh—truly laugh, until his sides ached—and his heart swelled. With her, he never needed to hide, or pretend; he could unfurl himself and be a better man because of it. He only hoped it was a fair exchange, and that he'd been able to bring her even a fraction of the happiness she'd gifted him.

He reached for the car keys in his jacket pocket and turned over the leather keyring to look at the picture slotted behind a protective piece of clear plastic, beneath which was written, 'ANNA & RYAN'. It was a snapshot of the pair of them grinning like fools on their wedding day, walking barefoot along the beach at Bamburgh with the sun at their backs.

"Here, lad," Phillips said, carefully. "Drink this."

Ryan tore his eyes away from the picture and looked up at his friend, who held out a polystyrene cup.

"It's muddy sludge, masquerading as coffee—just the way you like it."

He took the cup between his hands but didn't drink.

"It's been two hours, Frank," he said.

MacKenzie had excused herself shortly before, to collect their daughter Samantha from school, so Phillips sank onto the chair beside his friend and put a fatherly hand on his shoulder.

"It'll take as long as it takes," he said. "The doc said it might take a few hours, and that's normal."

Ryan said nothing, and Phillips tried again.

"I don't know much, but I know that Anna's a born fighter," he said. "If anyone can come through this, she can."

Ryan leaned his forearms on his knees and stared at the floor between his feet, every muscle in his body taut and poised for action.

"When I find whoever did this to her, they're going to wish they'd never been born."

There was a note to his voice that Phillips hadn't heard for a very long time—not since his sister's death.

"We don't know exactly what happened, yet," he cautioned.

"A cathedral that's stood firm for over a thousand years doesn't suddenly self-combust," Ryan growled. "This wasn't an act of God, or bad luck. Somebody had a hand in this—they must have done—and I'm telling you, Frank, there won't be a hole deep enough, or a corner dark enough for them to hide in, by the time I'm finished."

Phillips cast a worried glance in his direction, and then up at the clock on the wall, where the minutes continued to tick slowly by.

"Whatever happens, I'm your man," he said, and meant it.

CHAPTER 6

The stench inside the forensics tent was almost unbearable. Though it had been less than three hours since Tebbutt died, the process of decomposition had accelerated thanks to the unseasonably warm weather and the greenhouse effect wrought by layers of plastic sheeting. Consequently, when Lowerson and Yates dipped inside, they were met with a wall of hot, putrid air.

"Bloody hell," Jack muttered, from behind the protective mask he wore.

Tom Faulkner, the Senior CSI attached to Northumbria Police Constabulary, looked up from where he was crouched beside Tebbutt's inert body and surveyed them both from behind a pair of safety goggles. Like them, he wore polypropylene overalls and a hood, which did little to reduce the general temperature in the confined space.

"Hello," he said, in a muffled voice. "I was expecting to see Ryan and Phillips."

"Ryan's had some bad news," Lowerson said. "There was an incident at the cathedral, and Anna was caught up in it. He's at the hospital with her, now."

Faulkner's eyes widened. He'd worked with Northumbria CID for many years, and he considered Ryan a friend.

"That's terrible," he said, rising to his feet. "I knew there'd been an explosion—the rest of my team is over there now, waiting for the go-ahead to start sweeping. I had no idea…"

"We're stepping in, temporarily," Yates said, bringing them back to the matter in hand. It did no good to dwell on things they couldn't change, and they had a duty to Joan Tebbutt. "What can you tell us, so far?"

Faulkner gave himself a mental shake, then turned back to the unfortunate soul lying at his feet. She lay in a wide, cruciform position with her arms outstretched, half-in, half-out of the open front doorway so that her legs dangled onto the pathway while her torso remained inside the hallway beyond.

"Ah, well. Let's see…two shots have been fired. One grazed her neck here"—he stepped carefully around her legs to indicate a drag mark on the greying skin of her neck—"and hit her front door."

The tent was three-sided, covering the open doorway from public view but leaving the inside of the house accessible to the CSIs, who shuffled around the hallway searching for minute clues. Lowerson and Yates followed the direction of Faulkner's gaze to see the fresh, bullet-sized hole which now marred the paintwork.

"We've recovered that bullet, which we'll send on for ballistics testing," he said.

Lowerson hardly needed to enquire about the second bullet, for it was plain to see that it had pierced Joan's skull directly between her eyes, which remained wide open.

And staring.

He took a couple of long breaths between his teeth, while he fought the sudden wave of nausea. Despite having seen quite a few bodies, by now, they still had the power to affect him.

Yates, on the other hand, continued to look calm and collected.

"Were you able to recover the second bullet?" she asked.

It mattered, because, if the bullets didn't match, that increased the chances of there having been more than one assailant.

But Faulkner shook his head.

"It's still lodged in her brain, so that'll be one for the pathologist," he replied. "Judging from the way she's fallen, I can tell you there was sufficient velocity to throw her body backwards following impact, which is why her arms are outstretched. That would be consistent with the size and density of the bullet we've recovered. However, judging by the fact there's no exit wound, whichever weapon caused this wouldn't have had the same level of impact as, say, a police firearm. Besides, the bullet doesn't match the standard Glock 17 semi-automatic."

"The first responders say a couple of the neighbours heard a motorbike, followed by a couple of loud 'pops'," Yates said. "There are fresh, single-tyre tracks on the road that corroborate those accounts. That suggests an execution-style killing."

"You're thinking this could be gang-related?" Faulkner said, and just stopped himself from rubbing an itch on his nose. "Numbers are generally down after the Smoggies were cleaned out."

Until Operation Watchman, the Smoggies had been the ruling gang in the North East, and one of the most powerful in the country. Though they'd been able to put an end to much of their operations over the past few months, change didn't happen overnight. It was possible—more than possible—that Tebbutt had marked herself for murder.

"Numbers might be down, but there are plenty who would want retribution—for loss of business, honour, revenge…or, all of the above," Lowerson remarked. "Have you found anything else?"

"We found her car keys just there," Faulkner said, pointing to a small yellow marker inside the hallway. "Probably had them in her hand as she was leaving the house, and they were thrown wide as she fell. We arrived here shortly after the first report was made, so that will make the pathologist's job a bit easier, in terms of figuring out the post-mortem interval. As for the rest, we're going over the tarmac to take impressions of the tyre track, and obviously we'll look over the rest of the lane, too. It's possible they were waiting around a corner before driving past, or parked up a few doors along, so we'll see what we see. It'll be hours, yet, before we've finished going over the house."

"Do you need longer with the body?" Yates asked.

Faulkner had already taken extensive photographs, but a few more wouldn't hurt.

"I'm ready to turn her over, now. Once we've done that, I'll give you the signal."

And there, Lowerson thought, you had it. Fifty or more years of living and a career spent in public service, but it all amounted to being moved about like a piece of cattle meat.

"I need some air," he muttered, and stepped back out into the light.

CHAPTER 7

She was so pale.

Anna lay unmoving on the hospital bed, eyes closed and palms open, as though she was waiting to receive something, or to be received. Her skin was the colour of porcelain, highlighting the shadows beneath her eyes and the bruising which blossomed on one side of her face. They'd shaved the back of her head, robbing it of the long, dark hair she often left loose, leaving yards of surgical bandage in its place. Wires and tubes protruded from her skin and a heart monitor beeped at regular intervals.

Ryan listened to the sound of it, and watched for the slight movement of her chest, to reassure himself that she was still breathing.

Beep...beep...

"Mr Ryan? You can sit beside her, if you like."

One of the ICU nurses directed him to the single chair arranged near the bed, and he moved slowly, afraid to hurt her or dislodge something vital.

Here, he was no longer *Detective Chief Inspector,* but a man like any other—one who was afraid for his wife and child and fearful of the future, as yet uncertain.

Four hours after they'd taken her into theatre, Anna had been transferred to the ICU for observation. In the end, they hadn't needed to induce a coma because she still hadn't regained consciousness and, though they tried to sugar-coat it, the doctors were worried about the length of time it was taking for her to come around.

And so was he.

"Can she hear me?" Ryan asked.

The nurse looked at the tall, raven-haired man and felt her heart twist.

"Probably," she said. "Why don't you try talking to her?"

Ryan waited until the nurse had moved on, then shuffled forward and gently—very gently—rested his hand over Anna's cold fingers. It was like touching a butterfly's wing, he thought; too much force, and the skin might crumble.

"I…"

He cleared the constriction in his throat, absently rubbing the pad of his thumb over the wedding band on the third finger of her hand.

"I was worried about you, today," he said, in a stronger voice. "You know, it's funny. Every morning, as I leave the house for work, you tell me to be careful. But, today"—he swiped away sudden tears—"today, I was the one who was worried. I wish I'd been the one telling you to be careful, Anna. I wish it was me lying there, not you…"

His voice broke, as he watched her chest rise and fall.

"The doctors say they've stemmed the bleeding in your brain, darling, but they need you to wake up. It's important that you wake up, so they know if your speech has been affected or…or, anything else. And, I…I need you to wake up because I miss you, Anna. I need to hear your voice, so I know you're still—you're still with me."

The monitor continued to beep, but it was a comforting sound and he sat there for a few minutes listening to it, tracing the lines of his wife's face, before speaking again.

"You hurt the right side of your body, when you fell," he said softly. "You might be sore for a while, so there'll be no more scurrying around trying to do too much. Especially not with the extra pressure from the baby…"

The baby.

He wondered whether to tell her it was a girl. They'd been due to have their twenty-week scan, where the sonographer usually asks whether they'd like to know the sex of the baby, and hadn't really discussed whether it was something they'd rather keep as a surprise. Yet, it felt wrong to have the answer and not share it with the person who had the most right to know.

"In case you're worrying about the baby, it's fine," he said, and placed his other hand carefully on top of the bump protruding through the hospital bedsheets. "Anna, they told me it's a little girl. I hope you don't mind knowing…maybe it'll help you to imagine what she might look like."

Tears swam, but he swallowed them and carried on, determined to keep talking for as long as he could.

"I imagine her just like you," he whispered. "A dark-haired beauty, with big brown eyes. I hope she has your generous heart, your capacity for love and your intelligence—"

Just then, he felt a kick against his hand.

Ryan stared at the bump, holding his breath as he waited, then smiled when the baby kicked again.

"Hello, little one," he murmured. "We're so excited to meet you, but your mummy isn't very well, so I need you to be gentle with her."

He stayed seated like that, hands outstretched, for a long time. Then he leaned over to bestow the gentlest of kisses.

"I'll be waiting for you, whenever you're ready," he murmured. "Take as long as you need. I love you, Anna."

Phillips watched for a moment or two from the doorway, before retreating into the waiting room. Some things weren't meant to be shared, and it was enough for Ryan to know that he wasn't far away.

He'd never be far away, when help was needed.

* * *

Samantha had learned much from the first part of her childhood, spent with a travelling circus community. The first was seldom to place your trust in another person but, if you did, always, *always* to trust the language of their body and not the words that came out of their mouth.

Words were cheap, and easy to say.

Actions were harder to fake.

"How was your day at school, sweetheart?" MacKenzie asked, as they sat down to dinner.

There it was again, Samantha thought. The words were the same ones she used every night after school, and the tone was similar, but something was different. Denise, the woman she'd come to call *Mum* seemed distracted, her mind elsewhere.

It was different to the kind of distracted she and Frank sometimes got, when they had a big case at work. Then, they were, sort of, energetic…as if they couldn't wait to try and solve it. But this time was different.

Something was different, and she didn't know what.

"Fine," Samantha mumbled, pushing fishfingers and chips around her plate. "Where's Frank?"

MacKenzie looked at her, checked her watch, then got up to put the kettle on.

"He's working late," she lied.

Samantha frowned.

"I thought he was going to do some training with me this evening," she said, stubbornly. Lately, she and her adoptive father had been sparring together in their garage gym, and they both looked forward to it—she, to learn new boxing skills and he, to be reminded of his younger days.

"Well, I'm sure you can pick things up again tomorrow—or soon," MacKenzie amended quickly, thinking that none of them knew how long Anna would be in hospital nor what arrangements would need to be made.

Her shoulders slumped as she worried for her friends.

"How soon?" Samantha prodded.

MacKenzie sighed, and turned back to the girl, wondering what the books had said about hormone bursts happening around her age.

"Sam, I don't know how soon. We'll just have to see. You *know* our jobs can be a bit unpredictable, but one of us will always be here for you."

"Why don't you come and do it, instead?" Sam insisted. "You know all about kickboxing—Frank told me. Why don't you show me some moves?"

MacKenzie managed a smile.

"I would love to, but I'm not feeling up to it, today."

Her bad leg was hurting again, as it often did these days. The scar tissue—where a madman's knife had once pierced muscle and skin—was tight and hard, causing severe cramp throughout the day. It was a source of personal sadness that, as a very active woman, she wasn't able to do half the things she'd once enjoyed.

But she didn't mention that—it would only worry Samantha.

"Fine," the girl said, huffily, letting her knife and fork clatter onto her plate. "I'll just do it, myself."

"No, you won't," MacKenzie said, and there was a warning tone in her voice, now. "The gym is out of bounds unless you're supervised, as we've told you, before. There are lots of other things you can do before bedtime. Why not read a book?"

Samantha loved to read—usually.

"I don't want to read," she muttered.

"I don't know why you're in this mood, but you need to snap out of it," MacKenzie said, annoyed to hear the emotion in her own voice. "We could watch some television, for a while?"

But the girl pushed back her chair and stalked out, and a moment later Denise heard angry footsteps stomping upstairs.

On any other day, she'd have followed and given their new charge a few home truths about good manners and appropriate behaviour. But today…

Today, she couldn't seem to find the strength.

Tantrums and tears paled into insignificance beside the anguish Ryan must be feeling, and the worry that he might have lost Anna and the baby.

She sank down onto a chair and placed her mobile phone on the kitchen table in front of her, willing it to ring with good news.

When it did, she wept softly in profound relief.

She didn't hear the soft footsteps of the little girl, once unwanted and unloved, padding back to her room.

CHAPTER 8

Tuesday, 17ᵗʰ March

Anna awakened to a world of pain, and a view of the damp-stained ceiling tiles above her head.

Everything seemed to hurt, from her legs all the way to the torn pads of her fingertips—but especially her head, which felt heavy and sore, as though a vice were compressing it from either side. She blinked a few times, trying to clear the cloudy film across her eyes, and tried to swallow, finding the action difficult.

She closed her eyes again to rest them for a moment, the dim lighting on the ward proving too much, and listened to the humming sound of machines, and the beeping of a heart monitor.

Hospital? she thought. *Why?*

She tried to turn her head to look around, but the action brought a sharp, piercing pain to the right side of her neck and she let out a soft cry. The noise was enough to alert Ryan, who had drifted off in the stiff-backed chair beside her bed sometime after four. He was instantly awake and on his feet beside her.

"*Anna?* Anna, I'm here…it's Ryan, I'm here. Nurse!" he called over his shoulder. "Nurse!"

His face blotted out everything else, even the pain, and Anna gave a lopsided smile.

"Can you speak?" he asked, and then it occurred to him that her throat might be dry. "I'll get you some water—"

She let out a rasping sound, unwilling to let him go far.

"Wa—"

He turned back. "What did you say, my love?"

She looked up into his beloved face and wondered why he looked so scared, then remembered she was in hospital.

"Wh—wh'm here?"

She gave a slight shake of her head, moaning at the dart of pain, and wondered why she couldn't form the words.

The nurse rushed in, and Ryan moved back to allow her to step forward. Though the woman had a kind face, Anna's eyes grew wide and frightened.

Why wouldn't anybody tell her what was happening?

Was it the baby?

She tried to raise her hand to touch her stomach, but it seemed that her arm was made of lead.

"All her vitals look good," the nurse said. "I'll go and get Mr Barker."

At the sound of retreating footsteps, Ryan's face reappeared, and Anna felt his warm hand cover hers. His eyes shone like silver beacons in his tired face, and she wondered what could have been so bad to cause him to look so grave.

"Wh—apn'd?" she asked.

Ryan heard her slur, but he forced a smile onto his face. The most important thing was that she was alive and lucid.

She'd come back to him.

"You were hurt," he reminded her. "At the cathedral."

It took a couple of seconds, and then snatched images began to rain down as the door to her memory was thrown wide open.

Smoke…screams of terror…the explosions…

The cathedral…

"Cath'rl," she said, brokenly, and couldn't understand why Ryan looked shocked, before his face crumpled into laughter.

"You nearly died," he said. "I nearly lost all that's precious to me in the world, and you're worried about a few old stones and some mortar?"

He shook his head.

"Once a historian, always a historian."

The look she gave him told him clearly that she thought he was a heathen, then the worry crept back.

"Baby," she said clearly.

"Alive—and kicking," he added, with a smile.

She closed her eyes again, this time to rest.

* * *

"By God, lass, you gave us a hairy moment, back there!"

Phillips' booming voice could be heard down the corridors of the ICU and far beyond, but nobody seemed to mind.

"Sorry," Anna managed.

"Don't be daft," Phillips said, more softly this time. "D'you know how glad we are, to have you safe and sound? Just don't go giving me another fright like that, anytime soon. My old ticker can't take it."

She gave a weak smile, and noticed that he bore the look of a man who hadn't slept in his own bed, which he hadn't. Thanks to a liberal application of his legendary charm, Frank had been given special dispensation to spend the night draped over three of the chairs in the waiting room, so that he could be on hand, should his friends need him.

Ryan watched their byplay and felt warmth seep back into his veins.

Anger followed on swift wings, coursing through his body like white lightning.

Somebody might have taken this from him, robbing a woman of her life—and, not just any woman.

His woman. His wife. His love.

"—Ryan?"

He glanced up to find Phillips had asked him a question.

"What's that?"

"I was just saying, as soon as Anna's well enough, how about we all take a nice trip to Bamburgh?"

"Mm, lovely," Ryan said.

Phillips heard the note in his voice again, and judged it time for a man-to-man chat.

"Mind if we go and get a coffee, love? Can we get you anything?"

Anna shook her head, very carefully. She might have suffered a blow to the head, but she wasn't blind. She could see that Ryan had suffered a different kind of torment and needed to walk it off.

"Choc'l't," she said, as an afterthought.

"There's a girl after my own heart," Phillips winked. "Let me see what I can rustle up. C'mon Ryan."

"I'd rather stay here," he said.

"The nurse might want to give Anna a bath, lad," he murmured, leaning down to speak quietly in his ear. "Give the lass some privacy, eh?"

Ryan hadn't thought of that.

"I'll only be down the hall," he told her.

She gave him a reassuring smile, and a knowing glance for Phillips which told him clearly that she knew very well that he was a wily old fox.

* * *

Phillips managed to persuade Ryan to venture as far as the hospital canteen, whereupon he went about the urgent business of locating bacon sandwiches and chocolate mousse, for Anna.

"She probably can't swallow very well, so we need to be careful," he said to Ryan, who trailed behind him with a tray.

Phillips looked him over with a critical eye.

"Better make that extra bacon," he told the waitress, who nodded sagely.

Once seated, he thrust a plate in Ryan's direction.

"Eat," he said sternly.

Ryan lifted the sandwich in his hands and looked at it with a murderous expression, before lowering it again.

"Frank, they say there's still a possibility she could lose the baby. They're keeping her in for observation so she can rest, but I'm staying with her. I don't want her to be alone."

Phillips cleared his throat.

"And what does Anna want?"

"What do you mean?"

"Well," Phillips said, taking a healthy bite of his own sandwich. "Seems to me, she's out of the woods and needing to rest up. She'll be doing a lot of sleeping in that time, so what are you planning to do? Watch her while she dreams?"

He had, as a matter of fact, but when Phillips put it like that…

"What if she wakes up, needing something?"

"That's what the nurses are for and, besides, they're talking about moving her from the ICU to a general ward. That's an excellent sign."

"She might be lonely."

Phillips took another thoughtful bite, and realised that his friend was speaking of his own loneliness.

"Anna's on the mend now, son—you can see that, just by looking at her. There's a way to go yet, but she's got a bit of bloom back in her cheeks."

That was true, Ryan thought, and yet…

"When I think of whoever did this, I want to tear them, limb from limb."

He clasped his hands together and forced back the rage bubbling so close to the surface.

"Aye, I know," Phillips said quietly, wiping his hands on a napkin.

"Have you heard anything—from Morrison, I mean?"

Phillips shook his head.

"She knows not to disturb," he said.

Ryan said nothing, his eyes boring into the wall behind Phillips' head, where a television bleated the morning news.

"Around lunchtime yesterday afternoon, explosions shook the ancient cathedral, here in Durham. A cordon remains in place, and access has been denied to all members of the public whilst enquiries are very much ongoing. Specialist engineers have been drafted in to secure the central structure of the building, which is over a thousand years old, but authorities have yet to comment on the fact that priceless artefacts have not yet been removed for safekeeping. It is understood that there was one serious casualty and a number of people who suffered smoke inhalation, but no fatalities…"

Ryan flicked his eyes back to Phillips.

"Did you hear that? They reported on the cordon, the architectural stability of the bloody cathedral and its *artefacts,"* he sneered. "My wife and our baby get third billing."

He shoved back from the table.

"Morrison told me they're up against it in Durham Major Crimes—that's why she wanted to draft us in. There won't be anybody with the experience needed to handle an incident of this scale, and time's ticking away. If the cathedral is still standing, there had to be another reason for the explosions."

"Could be a botched job," Phillips put in, and reached a surreptitious hand across the table for the uneaten sandwich.

Waste not, want not.

"There's a security team at the cathedral, and eyes everywhere. Whoever did this was professional enough to plan ahead and detonate without discovery. It seems unlikely they'd miscalculate and fail to damage the structure, if that was the intention."

"So, what do you want to do about it?" Phillips asked.

Ryan narrowed his eyes.

"You planned this all along, didn't you? You wanted to take my mind off Anna, so I would be focused on the case, rather than worrying about her and all that could still go wrong."

Phillips lifted his chin.

"Would I be so conniving?"

"Yes."

"Well, let that be a lesson to you."

* * *

Much to Ryan's annoyance, when they returned to his wife's bedside it became clear that Phillips was right—once again.

"You sh'd head home for a show'r," Anna said, enunciating each word carefully.

The surgeon had told them her speech might be affected following her operation, but she was determined not to be downcast.

"I don't want to leave you here alone," Ryan said.

"Won't be," she replied and, with impeccable timing, one of the nurses popped her head around the door to check if she needed anything.

Anna tapped the small pot of chocolate mousse and shook her head.

"It's f'r the baby," she said, with a smile that made Ryan's heart contract.

She looked across and caught the raw emotion on his face, which was almost as painful as the wound on her head.

"I only w'nt inside to use the loo," she said, and grew tearful. "I'm s'rry."

Ryan took his wife's hand between two of his own.

"It's not your fault. Try to rest—"

"W'sh I could r'mem'b'r everyth'ng," she said, unhappily.

"Was it busy?" Phillips asked, matter-of-factly, and drew a frown from Ryan which he studiously ignored. Anna was a capable, intelligent woman, who would soon start to feel helpless and impotent stuck in a hospital bed. There were many things outside of her control but, at least this way, she could feel that she was helping the police effort.

She screwed up her face.

"Yesh," she replied. "Big gr'p waiting t' go in, too."

Ryan saw the tears evaporate while she focused her mind and understood what Phillips was doing.

"Do you feel up to giving a statement?" he asked.

She gave a watery smile.

"I want to," she said. "But I might fall a'leep."

"That's enough for today," Ryan said.

But she shook her head.

"I was looking at Cuthb't's cross, when the s'plosions came. They w're so loud…" She gave a small shiver, and her hands crept up to cradle her belly protectively.

Ryan caught the action and felt a fresh wave of anger.

"Smoke was ever'where," she whispered. "I—I jus' couldn't see—I tri'd to get out—"

Tears leaked from her eyes, and Phillips reached for a box of tissues, which Ryan used to dab her skin, very gently.

"No more," he urged her. "That's enough, Anna."

This time, she agreed.

"Fin' them," she said softly. "Fin' them, b'fore they hurt anybody else."

CHAPTER 9

Ryan needed no second bidding.

He and Phillips left Anna in the capable hands of the ward staff for a short while and made their way out of Newcastle towards Durham. It was a city they both knew well, particularly as Ryan had lived with Anna in the cottage she used to own there, down on the scenic banks of the River Wear. It had been a privilege to awaken each morning to what must surely be one of the finest views in the world and, at times, he missed it. It was a fairytale skyline, bringing to mind images of elven cities in fantasy novels, too beautiful to be real. Each morning, he'd watch the dawn rising up over the towers of the cathedral and marvel at the perfect pairing of Man and Nature. He remembered the sweet, dewy scent of the greenery on the riverbank, and could still hear the buzzing of insects in the marshes as he'd taken his daily jogs along the pathway that ran parallel to the water, which shimmered molten silver as it rippled towards the sea.

If he chose to, he could still remember the taste of that water.

The small scar on his abdomen throbbed—a phantom pain to remind him of the time he'd suffered a knife attack, and had been thrown into the river to die.

Ah, memories.

"Might be easier to walk from here," Phillips said, providing a timely interruption as they approached a multi-storey car park not far from the train station. "Traffic cops must have set up a diversion away from the centre."

Ryan agreed, and a few minutes later they parked up and made their way along the path beside the river until they reached the Silver Street Bridge. It was another fine day, and the many small shops and restaurants on either side of the bridge were brimming with customers, who seemed frankly undeterred by the news of a suspected terror attack.

"It must be nearly time for the students' Easter break," Phillips remarked, as they crossed the bridge. It was common knowledge that relations between the transient but lucrative student population, and the permanent residents of the city and its surrounding villages, was not always frictionless. Middle-class students brought deeper pockets, which had driven housing and retail prices higher for their working-class neighbours. Moreover, theirs was a different tribe of so-called intelligentsia—thus far, lacking in basic sensibilities and understanding of what constituted real life—and when a large number of residents were so wholly tone-deaf to the situation of their fellows, there was bound to be social tension.

"That'll come as a relief to some," Ryan said, acknowledging the problem, whilst privately admitting he'd been a part of it, in his earlier years.

Before joining the Police Training College, he'd completed an undergraduate degree at Cambridge, much to his father's chagrin—four generations of Ryan men had studied at Oxford, and it represented a break in tradition, such as it was. With the folly of youth, he'd believed himself to be a pioneer of sorts; a renegade, black sheep of the family, who'd made it on merit alone.

The arrogance of his former self was, to this day, a source of shameful embarrassment.

Looking back with the wisdom that came with age, he saw how blind he had been, living inside that privileged bubble. He wondered how many times he'd walked past a person in need of food or shelter, who'd been surviving on the cold outskirts while he'd enjoyed a charmed existence. He thought of all the times he and his friends had punted on the river or picnicked on the college lawn, their minds free of trivial concerns such as where their next meal might be coming from.

It made him cringe to think of it.

It might have taken time, Ryan thought, but he'd found his way in the end. Slowly, the veil had lifted. He'd seen inequality so stark, the food on his tongue became ash; division so wide, the clothes on his back felt like chains. Offers of respectable careers in the City had poured in, but he'd turned to a life of public service and, despite all he had seen and all that he'd lost, Ryan had never once regretted his decision.

"You look miles away," Phillips said, and they paused to stand overlooking the water, resting their arms on the warm stone walls of the bridge. "Penny for them?"

Ryan raised a hand to shield his eyes from the glare of the mid-morning sun.

"I was thinking about when I was their age," he said quietly. "What were you doing, when you were nineteen, Frank?"

Phillips ran a thoughtful hand over his jaw, and tried to cast his mind back over thirty years.

"I joined the Force when I was eighteen," he said, with a light shrug. "We were dealing with the Miners' Strikes around then, and the riots. I'd met Laura, and we were courtin'."

Ryan smiled at the old-fashioned turn of phrase Phillips used to describe his first wife, who'd sadly passed away from cancer several years ago.

"You know what I was doing, Frank?" he murmured. "Larking about on a river, somewhere, getting pissed."

"Well, there used to be a boat down on the Tyne," Phillips recalled. "The Tuxedo something-or-other, which they made over into a nightclub. We had a few laughs on there, so it's not all that different."

Ryan turned to look at his friend, a man he considered his better in so many ways. He couldn't count the times Frank had taught him humility with no more than a look, or a word, over the years they'd known one another, and he decided to chalk this one up on the tally.

"Come on," he said. "This case isn't going to solve itself."

"Lead on, Macduff."

* * *

A cordon had been set up in a wide perimeter around the cathedral, blocking the entrances from all sides, as well as access to Palace Green from the north, restricting access to the cathedral, castle, library and college buildings belonging to the university. Smaller businesses which fell within the designated area had also been forced to close for the day, which made for a number of disgruntled proprietors as well as several disappointed tour guides. A significant police presence had been drafted in to guard the cordon and repel any unauthorised visitors, including the press hounds who'd been there since first light, sniffing for an update in time for the late morning news.

"People just go on that whatdoyercall it, these days," Phillips said.

Ryan waited for further elucidation, but none was forthcoming.

"The 'whatdoyercall it'?" he asked, as they hiked up Saddler Street towards the summit upon which the cathedral had been built.

"Aye, you know. That…*Twatter*, or whatever it's called."

Ryan's lips twitched.

"Twatter?" he repeated.

"That's the one. People don't bother watching proper news, these days. They just go online to see all the videos people have recorded. How can a proper journalist compete with that, if you've got Mr and Mrs Nosy Parker filming everything in real time?"

Ryan was still reeling from Phillips' mispronunciation, but didn't bother to correct it because he had a damn good point.

"They can't compete," he said quietly. "People can film what they want and upload it, without any thought or feeling, and the damage is done. Politicians can say anything and be believed, because nobody's doing the fact-checking or, if they are, it comes too late. It's harder to claw words back, once they're out there, circulating in the world."

In their profession, Ryan and Phillips took a cautious approach to the press, having met several reporters over the years who employed a laissez-faire attitude towards rigorous, investigative journalism. Quick, easy and factually-questionable soundbites might be *de rigeur*, but that wasn't how things worked in Northumbria CID. All the same, they retained a healthy respect for a free press and what it could sometimes offer during the course of a long-running investigation, and they had no wish to create enemies.

Consequently, they skirted around the pack of reporters baying at the edge of Palace Green and dipped beneath the police line before they were spotted.

"Hey! You two, stay back, please—"

One of the constables ran over to reprimand them but, luckily—or, unluckily, depending on the point of view—Ryan's face and reputation preceded him.

"Sorry, chief inspector, I didn't recognise you, at first."

They showed him their warrant cards, always keen to observe the proprieties.

"I'm looking for DS Carter?" Ryan said, slipping the card back into his pocket.

"He's inside, sir," the constable said, and pointed towards the north door. "You can go through there."

"Do we need any safety gear?" Phillips asked. As they'd approached the cordon, he'd been surprised by the lack of hard hats on display, considering the level of threat less than twenty-four hours before.

But the constable shook his head.

"The structural engineers have already given the all-clear," he said. "Once the CSIs have finished going over the place, we'll be reopening to the public."

"We'll have to see about that," Ryan said, delicately emphasising the fact that there was a new SIO in charge, now. "You're doing a good job here. Keep it up."

"Thank you, sir," the young man beamed.

There came shouts from the other side of the line, as they were spotted by a reporter.

"DCI Ryan! What can you tell us about the explosion, yesterday? Do you believe there's a link to the bridge explosions in Newcastle, last year? DCI Ryan!"

Last year seemed like a lifetime ago, he thought, as they turned away and made swiftly for the north door.

* * *

Not being a man disposed to any religious bent, Ryan had only been inside Durham Cathedral a few times before—mostly, to accompany Anna. If his mind was not so frequently occupied by the faces of all the dead he'd failed to avenge, or cluttered with the day-to-day responsibilities of running the Major Crimes Unit, he might have taken a keen interest in local history. He'd never be able to match his wife's obsession with pagan folklore, nor her delight in uncovering fresh clues to the past, but he appreciated history for its uncanny ability to inform the *present*.

After all, there was very little that was new under the sun.

Likewise, he was no artist, but Ryan could recognise artistry when he saw it and it was plain, even to the most untrained eye, that the lines and columns of the cathedral constituted a significant work of art. The temperature was cool inside its stone walls, which acted as an echo chamber and created a spiritual hush for those who came to lose themselves in prayer. The reverent atmosphere couldn't fail to impress.

"Gets me every time, this place," Phillips whispered, as they were admitted inside by another earnest constable. "They don't make 'em like this, anymore."

Ryan thought immediately of their new police headquarters and had to agree.

"Why are you whispering?" he whispered.

"Why are you?" Phillips returned.

Ryan huffed out a laugh.

"The design reminds me of Notre-Dame," he said, in his normal tone. "It's awe-inspiring architecture, which is obviously part of its purpose. All the same, I can't help but wonder how much it cost to build this edifice, while people in the surrounding villages starved."

"That's organised religion, for you," Phillips said, cheerfully. "The Church was mighty powerful round these parts, especially back in the olden days."

"I can see that," Ryan said, eyeing the buttresses and stained glass. Though he was more concerned with human life than any bricks and mortar, Anna would be relieved to know that the building she loved so much had remained intact—at least, from what they could see.

Which begged the question—*how?*

They left the central nave and made for the exhibition galleries, where they'd been told they'd find DS Carter, who'd been managing the investigation pending Ryan's arrival. They'd protected their feet with shoe coverings, donned nitrile gloves and were pleased to find the CSIs had created a plastic walkway through the display rooms, to preserve any trace evidence that might otherwise be lost. They followed the walkway—and a lingering smell of smoke—through a warren of rooms in the Open Galleries until they reached the Great Kitchen, which was where Anna had been found.

The Great Kitchen was a grand, imposing space with a high, rib-vaulted ceiling dating back to the fourteenth century. Where once it had been used to feed its Christian community, the room now formed part of an impressive exhibition space, devoted to the relics of St Cuthbert. In the centre of the room stood a large display case housing the wooden coffin used to transport Cuthbert's remains hundreds of years earlier, before they were eventually laid to rest in another part of the cathedral that had come to be known as 'Cuthbert's Shrine'. Several other large display cases had been arranged at intervals around the room, and Ryan's eye was drawn to one in particular, which appeared to have been damaged during the explosions. One of its sides lay in pieces on the floor, and whatever had once lain inside was long gone. There remained a faint cloudiness to the air inside the room despite its high ceilings, and Ryan experienced a surge of emotion as he imagined his wife lying there on the hard stone floor until the Bomb Squad found her.

If they'd arrived a few minutes later…

Shoving the thought aside, he scanned the area, noting a cluster of white-suited CSIs who worked with quiet focus, while another group of people had congregated near the exit. They consisted of three men and a woman and, whether it was the way they held themselves or the general cut of their jib, the younger two members of the group seemed to bear an invisible brand proclaiming them to be 'POLICE'. One of them—a man somewhere in his late twenties—noticed their arrival and stepped forward.

"DCI Ryan? DS Phillips? I'm DS Ben Carter," he said. "We were all so sorry to hear about what happened to your wife."

Ryan managed a brisk nod of thanks and then gestured towards the other people hovering in the doorway.

"Why don't you make the introductions?" he suggested.

"Of course," Carter said, quickly. "This is DC Justine Winter, my colleague from Durham CID."

She was young, no more than twenty-two or three, but had the serious and watchful expression they'd come to recognise in their fellow officers.

"Anything you need, chief inspector, Durham Major Crimes is at your disposal."

Carter turned to the remaining two members of the group.

"We were just speaking with Derek Pettigrew, who is the Chief Operating Officer, with day-to-day oversight of the cathedral."

Pettigrew was a man in his late forties who looked as though he hadn't slept well the night before, which was hardly surprising in the circumstances.

"Pleased to meet you, chief inspector," he said. "Dreadful news about your wife—may we ask how she's faring?"

The question might have been kindly meant but it was poorly timed, and had been delivered in the kind of snivelling tone that set Ryan's teeth on edge.

"As well as can be expected in the circumstances, thank you," he said shortly, turning his attention to the final member of the group.

"This is Mike Nevis, the cathedral's head of security," Carter said. "Mr Nevis is in the process of collating the CCTV footage from yesterday."

Nevis was, contrary to stereotype, a thin wisp of a man. In days gone by, security personnel might have relied on brawn over brains, but they were living in a new world nowadays; one where cybercrime could be more dangerous than the average snatch and grab.

"Pull together the footage from the last four weeks, if you can," Ryan said. "An incident of this magnitude doesn't happen on the fly—it takes weeks of planning. We'll be looking for the same face, or faces, reappearing periodically."

"We have many thousands of visitors at this time of year," Pettigrew said. "It won't be easy—"

"Leave us to worry about that," Ryan replied, in a deceptively calm tone.

He didn't care how long it took, nor how many times he needed to watch the footage. He'd find whoever had been the one to hurt his wife and child, and they would pay.

"Ah, I believe the cathedral only keeps footage for a couple of weeks, isn't that right, Mr Nevis?" Carter said.

Nevis scratched his balding head.

"Actually, we installed a new system not so long ago, which is linked to cloud storage. We should be able to go back as far as you need."

Ryan smiled.

"What happened over there?" Phillips asked, bobbing his head in the direction of the broken display case.

"Of course, you won't have heard," Winter said quietly. "The explosions were dummies—just smoke bombs, to create confusion."

He'd known it, Ryan thought. The minute he'd learned the cathedral was intact, he'd known there must have been another reason.

"What's been stolen?" he asked simply.

"The cross," Pettigrew said, miserably. "They've taken Cuthbert's cross."

CHAPTER 10

Ryan and Phillips stood a safe distance away from a modern display unit that had once housed the gold and garnet cross belonging to Saint Cuthbert. A placard gave some facts about the artefact, and featured a smaller image of the cross.

"It's priceless," Pettigrew said. "Irreplaceable."

Ryan's jaw clenched, and he was forced to look away while he battled to keep his anger in check. The man spoke of an inanimate object as *priceless* and *irreplaceable*, yet all Ryan saw was the catalyst for what could have been his wife's death and, with it, the death of the future they had planned together.

That, and only that, was irreplaceable.

"Why this piece?" he wondered aloud, casting his eye over the remaining treasures suspended in airtight cases. "Why take the cross, and not the…what's that?"

He pointed at a sword, its dull metal blade gleaming beneath a subtle spotlight.

"The Conyers falchion," Pettigrew told him. "Legend has it, Sir John Conyers slew the terrible Sockburn Worm, or dragon, with it. It's thirteenth century, engraved with the arms of the Holy Roman Empire on one side, and the arms of England on the other. Some historians believe it might have belonged to Richard Earl of Cornwall, who was Henry III's younger brother, and who became King of Germany and King of the Romans in the mid-thirteenth century. It's presented to a new bishop of Durham when he first crosses the River Tees from the south and enters his new diocese, and is a symbolic commitment of Durham to its faith."

"You mean they take this out of the case every time?" Phillips asked.

Pettigrew shook his head.

"No, they use a replica, just like the replica of the Sanctuary Knocker," he explained. "The real one is in the case, over there."

They all turned to see the iconic knocker, designed to ward off evil spirits in the shape of a 'hell mouth'.

"And, these are all...priceless?" Ryan asked.

Pettigrew nodded emphatically.

"We considered moving them," Nevis said. "But, with the security system still intact, and no structural damage to the cathedral—"

"It seemed unlikely they'd chance a second robbery, sir," Carter put in. "They'd know police would be crawling over the cathedral after what happened yesterday, for one thing."

Ryan had known criminals for whom the chase, the risk, was everything, but he happened to agree with the younger man's assessment.

"I agree, they'd be fools to chance coming back here again. Besides, they had time to break into more than one case, if they'd wanted to take the lot."

"Which brings us back to your question," Winter said, in her quiet, no-nonsense way. "Why take the cross, and nothing else?"

"Maybe they wanted the gold?" Carter suggested.

Ryan gave a distracted shake of his head.

"Gold is readily accessible," he said. "They could hit any number of jewellery shops and save themselves the drama. No, it's far more likely there's a private buyer who wanted that cross, somewhere on the black market."

And, if that was the case, their job just became much harder.

"I don't understand how it could have happened," Nevis said, clearly nervous about any ramifications there may be for his ongoing employment. "Those display cases are state-of-the-art."

"Where there's a will, there's a way," Phillips replied, and cast his sharp eye over the industrial plastic casing which now lay broken in several pieces on the floor.

"What do you know, so far?" Ryan asked.

"The explosions went off around noon," Nevis replied. "The alarm was raised shortly afterwards as people began to exit the building and all staff began to evacuate the premises, and a separate alarm went off when the casing was breached. Unfortunately, this wasn't picked up as quickly as might otherwise have been the case—"

"What's the procedure for evacuation?" Ryan asked, as an image began to form in his mind. "Every man for himself?"

"Not at all!" Pettigrew was offended. "We check all the rooms, to ensure nobody—"

He trailed off and flushed with embarrassment as he realised his blunder.

"Nobody is left, bleeding on the floor?" Ryan finished for him, very softly. "Certainly, not in the House of God."

"Visibility was very poor," Nevis put in, hurriedly. "It's possible the volunteers didn't see your wife."

"Anything's possible," Ryan agreed, and gave the man a smile that would have chipped glass. "What happened after you finished your checks?"

"Control Room received an alert linked to the cathedral's alarm system, at twelve-oh-four," Carter said, a bit nervously. "First responders attended the scene, arriving at around six minutes past. The matter was referred to me, as I was the senior officer on duty at Major Crimes, and I contacted the Bomb Squad and the Counter-Terrorism Unit. We were fortunate that two members of the Bomb Squad were already in the city and had kit available, as they were due to attend a training seminar at the university, so they were able to attend shortly afterwards— otherwise there would have been a delay waiting for them to travel from the Explosive Ordnance Disposal Unit based at Otterburn. They accessed the building at around quarter past twelve, sir."

"Swift action," Ryan was bound to say. "When—ah, when did they find—"

"Your wife was discovered at around twenty past the hour, sir," Winter said. "Paramedics were already in attendance, and she was transferred to hospital."

He nodded, only too able to imagine the scene.

"Where was she found?" he asked, turning to face the room.

"Very close to the display case, here," Carter said, moving to indicate a yellow marker not far away.

"How had she fallen? What direction?"

When an answer was not immediately forthcoming, he spun back around.

"It goes to motive," he explained. "Was she running away, or was she defending herself? Was the attack more likely to have been accidental, or intended to immobilise? Has a weapon been recovered?"

His eyes tracked over the worn stone floor, but he could see no large implements capable of causing the kind of damage Anna had suffered.

"She was found lying on her right side, in this direction," Winter stepped forward and used her arms to describe the motion. "The display case would have been at her back."

"We haven't recovered any weapons, sir," Carter added. "But we're still in the process of searching the cathedral."

Ryan was silent for a moment, visualising his wife turning, seeking out the exit. As she turned, she was struck at the back of her head, hard enough that she fell forward as a dead weight, snapping her right ankle as her body fell awkwardly to the ground.

"How many explosions?" he asked. "Where were the devices found?"

"The Bomb Squad recovered one device in here, in the corner over by those pillars," Carter said. "Another three were detonated in total, two of which were found in the nave, hidden beneath some of the pews. The other one was found beside the font."

"Seems as though they were mostly for noise and show," Phillips said, keeping a weather eye on Ryan's taut profile. "Was any other damage caused?"

"We're delighted to say, none whatsoever," Pettigrew replied, clasping his hands together in a manner that was vaguely distasteful. "There's been some slight chipping to the woodwork, but nothing a good joiner couldn't buff out."

"Well, that's a great relief," Ryan snarled.

His wife had just come through life-saving surgery, but so long as their bloody woodwork was alright…

"What's been done so far?" Phillips asked.

"The Dean has been informed, of course," Pettigrew said. "She's very concerned, and has asked to be kept informed—"

Ryan raised an eyebrow, then looked sharply at Carter and Winter.

"All staff and volunteers of the cathedral should have been interviewed, or be in the process of being interviewed," he said. "Is that underway?"

"We have begun the process, sir," Carter said, looking uncomfortable. "The Dean had a prior engagement yesterday, so we haven't had an opportunity to speak with him yet."

Ryan turned to face Pettigrew.

"What could possibly have been more important than speaking with the police, at a time when the cathedral had come under attack and, as it turns out, one of its most prized possessions had been stolen?"

"I am afraid the Dean was indisposed," Pettigrew said, with some dignity. "He isn't responsible for leading ordinary prayers in the Cathedral, and, as you know, I take care of the day-to-day administration. He can hardly be blamed for not having been available, and he's a very busy man, at the best of times."

Ryan was unconvinced.

"I want a full and complete list of all staff and volunteers associated with the cathedral," he told Carter and Winter. "I want everybody interviewed—I want to know precise movements and, wherever possible, timings."

"But—you can't possibly think anyone of us would have been involved?" Pettigrew stammered.

Ryan looked at him for a long moment.

"You said it yourself, Mr Pettigrew—thousands of people visit the cathedral. It's possible that a gang of professional thieves orchestrated this, but it occurs to me how much *easier* it might have been, for somebody who already knew their way around—don't you think?"

"Derek's right," Nevis insisted. "The staff here know how sophisticated the security systems are and, besides, nobody could get past me—"

"That's just it," Ryan interjected. "What better way is there to hide than in plain sight? You wouldn't notice a familiar face, because they'd be part of the fabric here."

Nevis fell silent, and the crestfallen look on his face told them it was not outside the realms of possibility.

"Chief inspector," Pettigrew said, recovering himself. "The people who work inside this cathedral and on behalf of its community believe in *Christian values*. It isn't possible that any one of them could have done this, nor been complicit in any way."

Ryan found himself wondering how many times over the course of human history actions and misdeeds had been excused on account of the perpetrator professing to follow religious ideals. And yet, as Samantha had learned at a very young age, talk is cheap.

"Very laudable," he said. "But, as somebody once said, to err is human. You say that cross was priceless, but somebody *was* willing to name a price, or it wouldn't have been worth stealing. The price was obviously sufficient incentive for person—or persons—unknown to risk their safety and the safety of others, not least my wife and child."

Ryan looked back at the spot where Anna had fallen, then back into the slightly myopic eyes of the Cathedral's Chief Operating Officer.

"I'll leave forgiveness to the Divine, Mr Pettigrew."

CHAPTER 11

For the second time in as many days, Jack Lowerson grappled with an overwhelming feeling of nausea.

During his time as a policeman, then as a murder detective, he'd seen plenty of things that turned his stomach and kept him awake at night.

However, it seemed there was always room for more.

"You alright there, Jack?"

The enquiry came from Doctor Jeffrey Pinter, Chief Pathologist attached to Northumbria CID and their long-time associate. He was a tall, lanky man in his early fifties, with an eclectic taste in music and a cheerful demeanour that belied his grisly profession. Lowerson didn't mind so much that *ABBA's* greatest hits were blasting out of the speakers in the hospital mortuary; he was more concerned with the odour emanating from the immersion tank at the other end of the room.

He cleared his throat.

"I'm fine," he said, making a valiant effort to sound nonchalant. "Ah, is that new?"

Pinter looked over at the tank.

"She's a beauty, isn't she? Not new anymore, mind you. I suppose it's been a while since we've seen you in here, Jack. Would you like me to show you how it works?"

Pinter began to move towards the tank, presumably to reveal its contents.

"Ah, no—no, we haven't really got time," Lowerson said. "Have we, Mel?"

But, to his horror, Yates was already making her way across the room to peer inside the shiny metal tank.

"Fabulous new design…" Pinter was saying, cranking a wheel mechanism at one end. "We use it mostly for teaching, you know."

"I suppose it's helpful for the university students to learn their anatomy," Yates replied.

"Yes, indeed. Embalming, dissection—"

Another minute, Lowerson thought, and he was going to embarrass himself.

"Ah, we really should get down to business," he said, making a show of checking his watch. "We're due to have a briefing later this afternoon."

"Are we?" Yates was surprised.

He didn't quite meet her eyes.

"Probably," he mumbled, and moved swiftly on before she could grill him further. "So, Jeff, what can you tell us about Joan Tebbutt?"

Pinter gave a light shrug and stuck his hands in the pockets of his lab coat.

"I've put her in one of the private examining rooms," he said, and began leading them along a separate corridor. "I wasn't well acquainted with DCI Tebbutt, but colleagues in County Durham speak very highly of her, so I felt it was only right and proper she should be afforded her own room."

"That's good of you, Jeff," Yates said.

To ensure the investigation into Tebbutt's death remained as independent as possible, the decision had been taken to use specialist services normally associated with Northumbria CID, rather than their counterparts in Durham. It meant that her body had been transported to the Royal Victoria Infirmary in Newcastle, where Pinter kept an office, and Faulkner's team of CSIs had management of the forensic crime scene at her home in Seaham, rather than a local crew. Though nobody wanted to say as much, the fact was, it reduced the chance of any information being tampered with from an inside source.

They were shown inside one of the smaller examination rooms, where a shrouded figure lay on a metal table in the centre. A computer monitor hummed on a desk pushed against one wall, while an industrial strength conditioning unit rattled somewhere above their heads, keeping the temperature chilly. There was little it could do to mask the odour of chemicals, but it was better than the alternative.

"Here she is," Pinter declared, as the door clicked shut behind them. "Are you ready to dive in?"

It was a fact universally acknowledged that Jeff Pinter had a unique, ill-judged turn of phrase, which they forgave on account of him being one of the best in the business.

Lowerson gritted his teeth.

When the shroud was lifted, the overriding sensation both detectives experienced was *sadness*; not for the cruel damage to the bodily shell Joan had inhabited in life, but for the emptiness her broken body left in its wake, now that her soul had departed.

"Joan was fifty-seven, and in excellent physical shape," Pinter said, and they could see that had been true. She'd been trim, with good muscle tone. "A couple of old breaks and scars—one, where she gave birth by caesarean section, as you can see."

They nodded, and thought of the woman's daughter, who they'd spoken with the day before to convey the unhappy news.

"Generally good diet, although I found something interesting in her bowel," Pinter said. "Looked to me like a small tumour, which I've sent away for further testing. There's no mention of it in her medical notes, so my guess is that she was unaware of it, when she died."

Bowel cancer was one of the most aggressive types of cancer, but she should still have been given the right to fight it and stand a chance of survival, Yates thought.

"We can check with her daughter," she said. "Anything else?"

Pinter sucked in a long breath, as if preparing to deliver a theatrical monologue.

"Time of death corresponds with the police reports," he said. "The temperature outside was warm, yesterday, so her ambient body temperature was also warmer than might otherwise be the case. Given the circumstances, we can be fairly certain that Joan died on or around twelve-fifteen, yesterday afternoon. I've sent off her blood work for analysis but, frankly, I don't expect anything out of the ordinary on that score. It's quite clear that the lady died from a penetrating, cranial gunshot wound."

With a bit of a flourish, he produced a retractable pointing device from his pocket.

"There were two gunshot wounds," he continued. "The first grazed her neck, here, without causing much more than a tear in the skin—"

He indicated the spot.

"If that had been the end of it, Joan would still be alive today. Unfortunately, the second bullet entered her brain through the frontal cortex, not far from the parietal gland."

Lowerson and Yates both nodded, neither wishing to admit they hadn't the faintest idea where to find a parietal gland, or many other types of gland, for that matter.

"Would it have made a difference, if the emergency services had arrived sooner?" Yates asked.

The conversation with Tebbutt's daughter was still fresh in her mind, as she suspected it would be for a long time to come, and she knew that, if it was her own mother lying before them on a cold metal slab, she would want to know.

But Pinter shook his head.

"When a bullet enters the brain, it's moving at a speed much faster than the speed at which bodily tissues tear. That means it pushes the tissues aside, like a pressure wave, creating a cavity three or four times larger than the diameter of the bullet itself. This pressure wave is what tends to be fatal to the central nervous system," he explained. "If the cavity reaches the deep midline structures of the brain, or the brainstem, this significantly reduces the chance of survival, which would never be terribly good in any event."

He paused, and looked down at Tebbutt with compassion.

"I'm sorry to say, in this case, the bullet created a devastating cavity in Joan's brain. It's likely she died almost instantaneously."

"At least there was no pain," Lowerson said softly.

"There's that, at least."

"What about the calibre of the bullet?" Yates asked, and Pinter produced a small, sealed evidence bag which he held out to her.

"I removed this from her brain earlier today," he said. "Thought you might like to see the bullet before I send it off to ballistics for further testing."

Yates took the bag in her gloved hands and peered through the clear plastic at the little chunk of twisted metal inside.

So small, she thought. Such a tiny thing, to reap such devastation.

"Does it match the other bullet Faulkner recovered from the scene?"

"This one is a 9mm," Pinter said. "I haven't had sight of the other one because it was sent straight to ballistics, but I understand it was the same size."

"Standard handgun," Yates said, and handed the bag to Lowerson.

"It's incredible to think that something so small could cause so much damage," he said, echoing her own thoughts.

"It's not the bullet that causes the damage," Pinter remarked. "It's the person who pulls the trigger."

With that, he pulled the shroud back over Joan's lifeless body, tucking it around her waxy skin as tenderly as he might a child at bedtime.

"There were no defensive wounds," he added, quietly. "She didn't stand a chance."

CHAPTER 12

Ryan left Carter and Winter to oversee the work of the CSIs and make arrangements to interview the staff and volunteers, while he and Phillips made their way back to the hospital to check on Anna. It had only been a couple of hours since he'd left her bedside but it felt considerably longer, especially having seen where she'd sustained her injuries. Whenever he thought of his wife lying injured and alone, he was overcome by an emotion that fell somewhere between impotence and rage.

"Howay, lad," Phillips said, giving him a gentle nudge out of the north door. "Let's go for a stretch of the legs, it'll do us both good."

"The only thing I need is to find the low-life behind all of this," Ryan said, and began striding across the lawn.

Phillips sighed, but whatever words of wisdom he'd been ready to impart were interrupted by shouts from the press corps, who remained just outside the police cordon on the far side of Palace Green.

"*DCI Ryan! Is it true you've been called in because the explosions were linked to the terror attacks in Newcastle last year?*"

"No comment," he ground out, dipping beneath the barrier.

"*If the terror attacks aren't related, why have you been called in from a different Area Command?*"

Ryan held the police line up to allow Phillips to duck underneath, resolutely holding his tongue while they buzzed like flies around his head.

"*Is it true that a police officer was gunned down yesterday afternoon, in broad daylight?*" they shouted.

"*Was the attack gang-related?*"

"*Do you believe the attack is connected to the recent fire at Notre-Dame?*"

Ryan and Phillips had almost made their way through the crowd, when a final question tipped the balance.

"*DCI Ryan, is it true that your wife was injured in yesterday's blast?*"

Clearly, this was news to some of the other reporters, who obviously hadn't thought to bribe any of the hospital staff in the area, and their excitement reached fever pitch.

"Just keep walking, lad," Phillips cautioned.

"*Isn't it true that your wife's family and, in particular, her father, were involved in the cult known as the Circle?*" the same reporter shouted. "*Is there any connection?*"

"What the hell is he implying?" Ryan snarled.

"Just leave it—" Phillips said, but the warning fell on deaf ears.

Ryan spun around to face them, eyes wild with grief and loathing. "You enjoy this, don't you? You feed off the drama and the heartache. Well, here are a few scraps for you to take away."

Eagerly, camera men switched their lights to red and reporters held out portable mics, ready to capture an impassioned statement from a man already beloved by their viewing public.

Ryan stood tall and straight-backed, his dark hair gleaming in the late morning sunshine, a physical embodiment of the hero they wished him to be. But, as he swept his gaze over each face in turn, there was only one in the forefront of his mind.

Anna.

He was no hero, he thought. He was a very ordinary man who did his best to protect those he loved and the people he served. He asked for no special treatment, nor expected any starry-eyed hero worship; all he hoped for was a long life spent with good people, at the end of which he might be able to look back without regret.

But, he realised, they didn't care to hear any of that. It was easier to play the role, and pretend he felt no fear.

"This was no terror attack," he said, and the crowd fell silent. "Terrorism is morally reprehensible, and something we will never tolerate. However, terrorists can at least lay claim to some system of ideology, however flawed it may be. Terror attacks are usually perpetrated for a reason—not one that you or I might ever consider acceptable—but a reason nonetheless."

He paused to let that sink in, before continuing.

"In this case, we are dealing with the *grubbiest* of criminal," he said, choosing his words with care. "This attack was not carried out by anyone believing in a cause, just robbers who value money more than human life. They planned and executed a robbery in which they managed to steal one of our region's most precious artefacts: Saint Cuthbert's cross is a thousand years old, and carries national historic and religious significance, a value too high for any material price. These things meant nothing to the men or women who desecrated the cathedral yesterday."

A muscle ticked in Ryan's jaw, but he forced himself to continue. He had started, so he would damn well finish.

"In their greed, these people thought nothing of striking down a pregnant woman," he said, and couldn't prevent the tremor in his voice. "They cared even less whether she lived or died. A number of other people sustained minor injuries as they tried to escape, and they are lucky those injuries were not more serious, and that they didn't happen to be in the wrong place, at the wrong time."

As he looked out across the sea of expectant faces, Ryan wondered whose shadowy face he would uncover, before all was said and done.

His next words were for them.

"To the perpetrators of yesterday's crime, I say this: whether it's today, tomorrow, or a year from now, *I will find you*. There won't be a hole big enough, or dark enough, for you to hide in. For every action, there is a price. You may believe that you have stolen something that is priceless," he said. "You also very nearly robbed me of something even more priceless. For that, you'll answer to the police and to the laws of this land—but first, you'll answer to me."

There was a stunned silence, and then the crowd was galvanised once more. They clamoured for attention, but Ryan merely shook his head.

"I have to get back to my wife and child."

* * *

Phillips was waiting a short distance away.

"You don't have to say it," Ryan muttered, as they made their way back towards the car park.

"Say what?" Phillips asked, innocently. "I wouldn't dream of saying that Morrison won't be happy when she sees the lunchtime news, for example, or that you've just laid down a challenge to a certain kind of maniac."

"Morrison asked me to manage the investigation," Ryan replied. "I'm managing it."

Phillips pursed his lips.

"Sounded to me like you were laying down a marker. Be careful, lad. We're not dealing with a gang of shoplifters, here."

Ryan stopped and turned to look at his friend.

"They might have killed her Frank," he said. "I want their heads on a stick."

"Aye, I know," Phillips said, and ran a calloused hand over his chin. "Fact is, if anybody'd hurt Denise, I'd probably feel the same—"

"*Probably?*" Ryan retorted. "I seem to recall you marching into a known gangster's office, without backup, ready to thump his lights out, back when Denise was hurt."

"That's as maybe," Phillips said, obtusely. "All I'm saying is, just make sure that the head on a stick doesn't end up being yours."

On which note, Ryan's phone began to ring.

"I always said there was a touch of the clairvoyant in you," he said, holding up the display.

It was Chief Constable Morrison.

Ryan looked at the display for a long moment and then, much to Phillips' dismay, clicked the red button to bin the call.

"I already know what she's going to tell me," he said, slipping the phone back into his pocket. "With Anna being a victim, she'll say I can't remain focused and that I'll have some kind of unconscious bias."

"Nobody would blame you, if you did," Phillips said. "But there are protocols—"

"Don't talk to me about protocols, Frank. Everyone in Durham is close to this case," Ryan said. "The attack is on the heritage of the city, and of this entire region, which means everybody's got an interest. The same applies to the Tebbutt investigation, because there isn't an officer within a hundred-mile radius who didn't have some connection with Joan, and who could swear they had an entirely unbiased interest in finding her killer. You and I both know that."

Phillips heaved a sigh, and then nodded.

"Aye, that's true enough," he admitted. "What'll you do about Morrison?"

"The Chief Constable can wait a little while longer," Ryan said. "If she wants me off the case, she'll have to come and tell me in person."

* * *

It was so beautiful.

Gleaming, with its polished gold and garnets; a pretty thing for anybody to behold. But this collector was no magpie, seeking out scraps of glitter. The beauty of the cross lay *within*, its power much greater than pounds and pence.

Their eyes strayed to the television, where the policeman spoke of things he could never comprehend, and the old anger began to rise, as it had since their earliest memories of childhood. Back then, it had been small things, trivial things, to some.

To ordinary people.

They'd always known they were special; set apart from the common herd. With such a bloodline, greatness of mind was more than a lifetime's achievement—it was preordained.

Fuelled by the knowledge, they reached for the cross with trembling hands, hesitating only for a moment before grasping it with greedy fingers.

The rush was incredible; the feeling of ecstasy so potent, their body shook with the force of it. They felt the power transmitting itself from vessel to master, as though it were touching their very soul, enriching every fibre of their body.

The cross was still strong, and so were they.

Reverently, they set the cross back down and stepped away, raising a hand to wipe away the spittle from their mouth.

This time, when they looked at the television, their eyes shone with madness.

CHAPTER 13

The journey back to Newcastle took longer than expected, and the delay did little to calm Ryan's nerves, which were already frayed by thoughts of all the worst-case scenarios that might have played out during his absence from the hospital. When he finally did arrive back at the Royal Victoria infirmary, the situation was not helped by the fact his wife was missing from her bed—which was now occupied by an elderly lady sporting a jazzy blue rinse.

"Are you looking for someone, pet?" she asked, in a frail voice.

"My wife," he answered, looking around for the nearest healthcare professional.

"My husband passed away last winter," the lady said, looking away for a moment to stare down at the tubes protruding from her hands. "If he was still here, he'd have come to visit."

Although he was distracted, Ryan took a moment to listen. Life was made up of small moments like these and, after all, he was lucky.

He was not alone.

"I'll be with him soon, no doubt," the woman continued.

Ryan wondered how best to answer. He didn't believe in an afterlife; only in the here and now. But he had no wish to belittle or deprive others of whichever belief system helped them through the day and, if the lady was seriously unwell, the thought of joining a husband she so clearly loved and missed would be a comfort.

He would be the last person to rob her of that.

"Do you have any other family?" he asked gently.

"A son and a daughter, but they lead busy lives, down south," she said, fussing at the bedclothes. "I'm that proud of them both. Our Tony's an accountant, and Sally's an artist."

"Do they know you've been unwell?"

Her mouth took on a stubborn line he found endearing.

"No sense in worrying them," she said. "I'll be out of here soon, and they'd have come all the way up here for nothing."

Presently, a nurse entered the room carrying a roll of fresh surgical bandages and a couple of glossy magazines tucked beneath her arm.

"Here we are, Mrs Kaye," she said cheerfully. "Let's get you freshened up. Would your visitor like to wait in the friends and family area?"

Ryan opened his mouth to say something politely to the negative, and to ask after the lady he was anxious to visit, but was pipped to the post.

"Oh, that's just my toyboy," the old lady said, with a twinkle in her eye.

"Is that so?" the nurse said. "I wondered why your heart rate seem to have picked up."

"Aye, well I'm not blind yet," Mrs Kaye said, and gave a wicked chuckle that soon descended into a coughing fit.

Ryan began to turn away, when a distant and long-forgotten memory of his grandmother came to mind. He recalled a precocious, if not downright cantankerous lady, with bright blue-grey eyes similar to his own—and a penchant for heavy perfume, pearls and hard Irish whiskey.

"I'll bring you some flowers next time," he said, with a smile, and then turned to the nurse. "I was looking for the lady who was previously occupying this bay. Anna Taylor-Ryan?"

"Oh," the nurse replied. "The lady who's expecting?"

He nodded.

"They moved her onto the main ward," she told him. "Two floors down."

Ryan thanked her and was about to hurry away, when some impulse made him turn to blow the old lady a kiss.

He was rewarded with a smile that stayed with him, warming his heart through the sterile hospital corridors until he found Anna again.

* * *

When Ryan was eventually reunited with his wife, he found that she was not alone.

A tall, silver-haired man with a chiselled profile stood at the shoulder of a petite, dark-haired woman of around sixty, who was seated in a faux-leather wingback chair beside Anna's bed.

"Mum? Dad? I had no idea you were coming," he said, leaning over to brush his lips over Anna's. She still looked pale, he thought, but better than she had earlier that day.

Watching him, Eve Finley-Ryan's face broke into a maternal smile and she rose from the chair, covering the distance between them to wrap her arms around him.

The tight ball of worry lodged deep inside Ryan's heart began to uncoil in the warmth of his mother's embrace, and he relaxed as she held him tightly against her.

"There," Eve murmured. "We came as soon as we could, and we'll stay as long as you need us."

"I don't need—"

Ryan began to pull away, to reject the help that was offered, an automatic denial on the tip of his tongue. There had been a time in his life, after his sister Natalie's death, when guilt and shame had driven him into isolation. He hadn't wanted to see the sadness in his mother's eyes—a sadness he was convinced he was responsible for. But now, he realised it had been a different kind of grief he'd caused—the grief felt by a mother who believed she had lost *both* of her children, when only one had died. Now, when his parents had come to support Anna and the baby—and him, too—he realised it would be only too easy to make the same mistake again.

So, instead, he accepted the hand that was held out to him.

"Thank you," he said.

Anna smiled, and he reached over to squeeze her hand.

"We're both very happy you're here."

Eve looked at their joined hands, and was overcome with love, and relief. Anna had been her son's redemption and, for that reason alone, would always occupy a special place in her heart. She, who had lost a daughter, had found a new one in the young woman who had lost a mother. Together, they had forged a special relationship, and she knew she had Anna to thank for bringing them closer together as a family.

"Frank rang us, late last night," she said. "We drove up, first thing this morning."

He might have known it would have been Phillips, Ryan thought. The man had firm ideas about family and, on this occasion, he had to agree with his foresight.

He looked over at the other member of their small gathering, who had yet to speak a word.

Charles Ryan was what Mrs Kaye might have called, 'a fine figure of a man'. In his late sixties, his father might easily have been ten years younger, with an athletic frame and a shock of steel-grey hair which had once been as dark as his own. After serving in the military in his younger years, Charles had spent much of Ryan's childhood and adolescence travelling, as part of his professional duties in the Diplomatic Service.

Now, Ryan felt, as he always did, that there was a distance between them; a chasm he longed to bridge, yet didn't know how. Whereas others like Phillips were easy with their affection, and never shy to administer a manly hug, his father seemed either unwilling or unable to do likewise. Consequently, he remained on the other side of the hospital bed, a physical reminder of the emotional distance between them.

Sensing the tension, Eve stepped into the breach.

"Why don't we go and get a coffee, Charles, and give Max and Anna some privacy?"

"Is it 'Max' anymore?" his father asked. "I understand we're supposed to call him 'Ryan' now."

There was an awkward, heavy silence, and Eve sent her husband a look which spoke volumes.

"Call me whatever you like," Ryan said, echoing the man's clipped, well-rounded tones. "As I recall, you often referred to me as 'boy', whenever you were at home. That will be more difficult now, since I'm no longer a boy and haven't been for some time."

"So I see," his father replied, and would have cut off his own tongue rather than admit how proud he was, just to be standing there looking at him.

He clasped his hands behind his back and walked to the door, stopping only to give Anna's hand a brief pat on the way out.

"Canteen's this way," he said, briskly.

CHAPTER 14

While Ryan grappled with family politics, it was Phillips' turn to do the school run.

Much like McKenzie, he had almost resigned himself never to experience the joys of parenthood—firstly, because he and his late wife Laura had been unable to have children, and, secondly, because it was growing late in the day to think of becoming a father by the time he found happiness with MacKenzie. Still, they'd been happy as a couple, he recalled, and life never felt lacking in any way.

Until Samantha had come into their lives.

Loving the little red-headed girl had proved as easy as breathing. Smart, sassy, and with a sweet tooth to rival his own, it was as though she'd been meant for them from the very beginning. True, the adoption process was not yet complete—and that gave him some bad moments when he allowed worry to creep in—but Samantha seemed happy, and had even taken to calling McKenzie 'Mum', sometimes. The house was a lot noisier with her in it, and there had been some minor run-ins as the three of them had grown to understand one another and live together, but, by and large, she'd slotted into their lives like the missing piece of a jigsaw.

He'd even grown to like the school run, something most parents dreaded each day. He supposed that, when your daily grind involved standing over dead bodies or chasing down low-lifes, being stuck in a bit of afternoon traffic didn't seem half so bad.

The playground was another matter entirely.

Although he'd heard rumours of other fathers doing pick-ups and drop-offs, they must have been a rare breed, since Phillips often found himself the lone male in a crowd of females, all of whom seemed to look alike. With the odd exception, they were all similarly dressed and appeared to frequent the same hairdresser, judging by their identical shades of blonde. It made him smile to think of McKenzie standing where he was now; with her vibrant hair and general air of capability, she'd stand out like a rare, exotic flower.

Which, he acknowledged, was exactly what she was.

Lost in pleasant thoughts of his wife, Phillips failed to notice the approaching footsteps until they were almost upon him.

"Detective Sergeant Phillips?"

He jumped, taken unawares by the arrival of the school's Deputy Headmistress.

"Aye, you're looking at him," he said, cheerfully. "Mrs Wilson, isn't it?"

She nodded, reluctantly shaking his calloused hand.

"I wonder if we might have a word," she said.

"What about?"

"I'm afraid there's been an incident," she said, in a tone that might have been used to hand down judgments in the Old Bailey.

"Aye, well, you're bound to get the odd bit of rough and tumble, even at a nice school like this," he said. "What's happened, then? One of the boys pushed my girl?"

If possible, Mrs Wilson's face grew even more stern.

"Not quite," she said. "Please, come into my office, where we can discuss the matter in private."

Phillips trailed after her, feeling like a dog about to be served his last meal as several pairs of eyes watched his progress across the tarmac.

* * *

It has been a long time since Phillips had found himself on the wrong side of a headmistress—although, in his day, they hadn't been averse to a spot of corporal punishment, regardless of whether the law had made it illegal to crack the cane. The memory of it stung his palms, and he clasped them together to try to rid himself of the sensation.

"What's happened, then?" he asked. "Has somebody hurt her?"

"Actually, Mr Phillips, it's the other way around. I am afraid it was Samantha who struck one of the other girls in the playground earlier this afternoon."

She paused, giving him another stern look, to drive the point home.

"Naturally, I don't need to tell *you*, this is hardly the kind of behaviour we expect from the children who attend this school."

Phillips almost remarked that, surely, the same could be said of *any* school, but decided to gloss over the point.

"What did this other lass do?" he asked.

"I beg your pardon?"

"Well, this other lass must have said or done something to provoke Samantha, so I'm asking what it was. Samantha knows not to hurt anybody, except in self-defence, so there must have been something to set her off."

The headmistress's lips flattened into a hard, disapproving line.

"There was *no* provocation whatsoever," she said, with some alacrity. "I must say, Mr Phillips, I'm surprised that someone in your profession would look for excuses—"

Phillips leaned back in the visitor's chair and linked his fingers over his paunch.

"Excuses, no. Justification, maybe," he said, mildly. "So, I ask you again, Mrs Wilson. What were the circumstances?"

The woman folded her arms, by now extremely put out to find he had no intention of making any instant or grovelling apologies until the full facts were known. In her experience, parents were only too eager to accept her final word, unwilling to challenge her authority.

That was the natural order of things, and she'd come to expect it.

In fact, she'd come to relish it.

"I understand the girls were playing together nicely during break time, until Samantha launched an attack on one of them, completely out of the blue," she snapped.

"Which girl?" he asked. "Were there any adult witnesses?"

She was starting to feel uncomfortable at his cross-questioning, especially when she hadn't thought to ask about other witnesses herself.

"There must surely have been a teacher on duty in the playground," he prodded. "Why don't we ask them in, and get the full story?"

Wilson turned a slow shade of red.

"Ah, we do have an…an attendant on duty," she said quickly. "Unfortunately, the area where this incident occurred was around the side of the climbing frame, where it's hard to see—"

Phillips' brows lowered, ominously.

"You mean to say, no adult saw the incident?"

"Well, no, but—"

"But?"

"One of the other girls saw the whole thing," she said.

"And, is she friends with Samantha or this other child?" Phillips enquired.

"She's…well, yes, she's the sister of the girl who was hurt."

He gave her a long look, and she shuffled uncomfortably in her seat.

"Samantha does not deny she hit the girl," Wilson said, with an attempt to regain her former authority. "I'll go and get her now, and have her explain the whole thing."

"Both girls, please."

She paused by the door.

"The other girl has already gone home," she said. "Samantha has been in detention for most of the afternoon—"

Phillips turned hot, then cold with anger.

"You punished my girl and let this other one off, scot-free, before you knew the full facts?"

"I used my discretion," Wilson said, swallowing nervously. "Samantha was the one to lash out—"

"Where is she?" he demanded.

* * *

When the headmistress returned with Samantha in tow, the girl's face was a picture of misery.

Phillips rose from his chair and curved a protective arm around her shoulders.

"Come and have a seat, and let's get to the bottom of this."

"Mrs Wilson probably already told you what happened," Samantha mumbled. "What else is there to say?"

Mrs Wilson let out a triumphant snort, which Phillips found highly inappropriate.

"See?" she said. "It's exactly as I told you—"

Phillips silenced her with a look, then turned back to his daughter.

"It's not like you to hurt anybody, Samantha," he said gently. "Are you sure nothing else happened? You can tell me anything."

The girl raised her head to look at him, and his eye was immediately drawn to a slight swelling on her bottom lip.

"What happened to your lip?" he asked.

In his peripheral vision, he saw the headmistress shuffle uneasily in her chair to get a better look.

"What's that?" she asked.

"Precisely my question, Mrs Wilson," he said. "Go on Samantha, tell us what happened."

Her eyes strayed across the desk towards a woman she found cold and unapproachable, then back to the man who had always been kind to her, and whom she had begun to think of as a father.

Phillips read the indecision on her face and was sorry for it. He'd hoped that he and McKenzie had given Samantha sufficient love and security to build trust between them, but then, he couldn't step inside the child's mind to fully understand the conflict within.

"I didn't want to do it," she said eventually. "But I had to make her stop."

"Make who stop?"

Samantha cast another dubious glance towards her headmistress, but drew strength from Phillips' steady gaze.

"She's called Francesca, and it happens every playtime. She trips me up, or pushes me, then says it was an accident—but I know it wasn't. When she thinks nobody else can hear, she calls me a dirty gypsy and says nobody likes me."

"Go on," Philip said, while his heart quietly broke.

Samantha was the orphaned child of a travelling circus community; a sensitive, intelligent girl who'd learned to live by her wits. She hadn't been given any formal education, and starting school behind everyone else had been a daunting prospect. She'd demonstrated courage and resilience, making friends and learning quickly—so quickly, it hadn't taken her long to catch up with the rest of them.

Perhaps that was the problem—maybe she'd seemed too happy, or too smart, and some little brat had decided to bring her down a peg or two, to make themselves feel better.

Phillips could understand human frailty, and had never considered himself infallible. But to think that anybody could be so cruel as to mock Samantha's heritage, or to laugh at her loss, was more than he was prepared to tolerate.

Add in the pushes and shoves, and he was ready to break some heads, himself.

"How long has this been going on?" he asked. "Have you told any of the teachers?"

"I tried—"

"I must interject," Mrs Wilson said. "I realise, Mr Phillips, that parenting is somewhat *new* to you"—she favoured him with a condescending smile—"however, it's very common for children who know they are likely to be disciplined for bad behaviour, to try to find a way to wriggle off the hook. They make up all kinds of tall tales, painting themselves as the victim. Now, Samantha, I'd like you to think *very* carefully before you answer the question I'm about to ask you. Do you understand?"

Samantha nodded.

"Are you sure you're telling us the full truth?"

Samantha looked up at Phillips with big, tearful eyes, and shook her head slowly. But, before Mrs Wilson could utter another word of self-congratulation, she said the words no headmistress wanted to hear.

"I haven't told you the full truth yet," she said. "That's because Francesca's mum is one of the teachers here, and she says nobody will ever believe me, not since all of the other teachers are friends with her mum."

Phillips thought how sad it was that children must learn at so young an age how corrupt the world could be.

Luckily, they could also learn that there were those willing to fight to make it better.

"How did you hurt your lip?" he asked again.

"Francesca barrelled into me when we were all playing tag. She made it look like an accident and said sorry *really* loudly, so everyone would hear and think she really was sorry, but she had a nasty look on her face. I don't know how else to describe it."

Phillips knew exactly what she meant. He'd seen similar looks on plenty of faces in his time.

"Did you tell anyone about it?"

"I knew nobody would believe me, so I didn't bother to say anything. Everybody thinks she's Miss Perfect, so what's the point?"

She gave a dejected shrug, and fell silent again.

"Truth is its own reward," Phillips said with a smile. "Hopefully, you'll have taught her a good lesson today, but, you know, some folks are a bit slow on the uptake. You be sure to teach this Francesca a thing or two about good manners, if she ever happens to accidentally barrel into you again, alright?

Samantha gave him a shy smile.

"Thanks, Frank," she whispered.

"We'll be going home now, Mrs Wilson," he told the headmistress. "I trust I have your assurance that, from now on, the playground area will be properly supervised, so that my daughter doesn't have to fend off any further bullying behaviour."

"I—"

He cut her off.

"I know that a woman in *your profession* wouldn't look to make any excuses for what's been allowed to happen here, today," he added, and the woman had the grace to look abashed. "Howay lass, I think this calls for some chicken nuggets from the takeaway."

"Really?"

He waited until they were outside in the school corridor before brushing a gentle knuckle over her cheek.

"Dinner of champs," he said, with a wink.

"Frank?"

"Yes?"

"Francesca said something else, too. She said…she said you weren't my real mum and dad, and that…that…you wouldn't want to keep me, because nobody would want a gypsy in their house. Is that why Mu—Denise was crying last night?"

Phillips dropped down onto his haunches in front of her, so she could see his face and read the truth of what he was about to tell her.

"Sam, first of all, let's never use that word 'gypsy' again," he said. "It has a pejorative—"

"What does 'pejorative' mean?" she interrupted him.

"Oh…it means, when somebody uses a word like 'gypsy' in a negative way, to hurt somebody else."

"Like, when somebody says a person from Sunderland is a 'mackam', and they say it in a bad way?"

They were getting into dangerous territory now, Phillips realised. Generations-old football rivalry between Newcastle and Sunderland had given rise to all manner of nicknames, which might have started out innocently enough but had since taken on some very unflattering connotations.

"Absolutely right," he said, and told himself to be more circumspect, in future. "That's a good example."

"Okay," she nodded. "So, we won't say 'gypsy' or 'mackam'."

He nodded.

"The next thing is even more important," he told her. "You might have heard Denise crying last night, and that's because Anna was hurt in the explosion at Durham Cathedral, yesterday."

"People were talking about it, today," she said.

"Yes. We were worried because she needed to go to hospital, and we weren't sure whether things would come right, in the end. We didn't tell you, because we didn't want you to worry, too, but I can see that's made you worry about other things, hasn't it?"

Samantha's eyes filled, and she nodded.

"Is Anna going to be okay?" she whispered. "And, the baby?"

Phillips smiled.

"Yes, I think so," he said. "She's spending another night in hospital, but Ryan's hoping to take her back home, tomorrow."

"Okay," she said. "Can I make her a card?"

"Aye, love. That would be nice." He thought of all he wanted to say, right there in the empty school corridor. "You're a treasure, Samantha. Anybody would be proud to have you as their little girl, but they can't, because me and Denise…well, we want you to be ours, if that's still alright with you?"

Her lip wobbled, and a tear spilled over as she nodded her head.

"Yes, please."

His arms drew her in for a warm, bear-like hug, and her voice was muffled against his shoulder.

"Frank?"

"Mm hmm?"

"Can I start calling you 'dad'?"

Phillips swallowed, his voice heavy with emotion.

"Anytime you like," he said, coming to his feet again. "And you can always tell us, if any little bugg—If any little girl or boy is bothering you. I'll teach you some nifty new moves to have in reserve, just in case."

As they set off down the corridor, he felt her small hand slip into his own and smiled at something Ryan had said the day before. Since he was now the proud father of a little girl, he'd have to start thinking about getting a shotgun of his own, one of these days.

CHAPTER 15

As the afternoon began to stretch into early evening, Ryan left Anna in the care of his parents and the hospital staff, and set off for Police Headquarters.

There was work to be done.

Conversation died as he stepped back into CID, and he decided now was as good a time as any to rip off the proverbial bandage.

"I—ah—I want to thank you all for your well wishes, yesterday," he said. "I'm pleased to say my wife and child have come through the worst, and we have reason to be optimistic she'll make a full recovery."

There was palpable relief all round, possibly more so because their leader had returned to something resembling his former self. However, Ryan knew there was one person to whom he owed an apology, and it couldn't wait any longer.

He found the Chief Constable in the break room, stirring a sachet of sweetener into a freshly brewed cup of tea.

"Do you have a moment, ma'am?"

She looked up briefly, then stirred her tea with more force than was strictly necessary.

"Well, if it isn't the prodigal policeman," she said. "You know, Ryan, we were all sorry to hear what happened to Anna. That doesn't give you the right to ignore protocols that exist for very good reason. Nor does it give you the right to ignore a senior officer for six hours on the trot—"

"I apologise unreservedly," he said, and her mouth fell open in shock. "My actions were both rude and unacceptable, and, although it's fair to say I was consumed with worry at the time, that isn't any excuse. It won't happen again, ma'am. You have my word."

Morrison took a bolstering sip of tea, finding herself momentarily at a loss.

"I'm glad you've come to your senses," she said. "As for you continuing to run the investigation into the robbery, that's obviously out of the question—"

"Respectfully, I disagree," he said.

"I knew it was too good to last," Morrison said, and took another sip of tea to hide her smile. "Ryan, you and I are both aware that, since Anna was caught up in the incident, that precludes you having any involvement without your judgment being compromised."

"Has my judgement ever really been compromised?" he asked, rhetorically, for they both knew he had a forensic ability to remain clearheaded, even in the most challenging of circumstances.

"Listen, the reason you called me in yesterday morning was because there isn't a senior officer with the experience to handle an incident of this scale at Durham CID. That's compounded by the ongoing investigation into Tebbutt's death, which may cast some doubt on her wider team. There isn't anybody who could be wholly independent—more so, because the cathedral means so much to the people around these parts."

He paused and stuck his hands in his pockets.

"In other words, you're saying you're the best I've got?" Morrison said.

"Not quite," he replied. "I've asked McKenzie to step in and take over operational control of the cathedral investigation, as acting DCI. We can work together from our base here, but I will defer to her judgment on operational issues at all times. This arrangement will allow me to focus my attention on the Tebbutt investigation, which is progressing well thanks to Lowerson and Yates."

Morrison regarded him with a thoughtful expression.

"You must be bloody infuriating to live with," she said, eventually. "You know, I was looking forward to a nice, old-fashioned barney. Then, you waltzed in here and took the wind out of my sails, with your apologies and your perfectly reasonable plans. Don't let it happen again."

"I apologise, ma'am," he said, grinning.

"Oh, bugger off," she told him.

"Actually, there's a briefing due to start in a few minutes," he said. "I'll cover the Tebbutt case, then hand over to MacKenzie. I wondered if you'd care to join us."

Morrison let out a long, rich peal of laughter.

"You set up a briefing, knowing full well I'd end up agreeing to all this, didn't you?"

Wisely, he remained silent.

"Fine. I'll be down in a minute."

He inclined his head and was about to leave, when she added, "I meant what I said, before. Give my best to Anna, won't you?"

"I will. Thanks, Sandra—for everything."

* * *

Despite Ryan's personal interest in the cathedral case, it was the Tebbutt investigation that took precedence in the briefing room, a short while later. A police murder would always be their number one priority, and Ryan knew he could have called upon any of the officers in his command to lend their help. However, given the sensitivity of the case and, in particular, Tebbutt's recent involvement in weeding out internal corruption, he decided to keep the numbers small and select.

He waited until Morrison had settled herself, then moved to the front of the room.

"Joan Tebbutt was an outstanding detective and an upstanding woman," he said simply. "Her death is an affront—not only to her, and to the family she leaves behind, but to every member of the Force. She was one of ours, and will be afforded every respect as we conduct ourselves throughout this investigation. Is that understood?"

There were nods of agreement around the room.

"Some of you may be wondering why I scheduled a briefing to discuss two separate investigations," he said. "The reason has to do with timing. Less than fifteen minutes after the explosions at Durham Cathedral, Joan Tebbutt lost her life."

He paused, letting that sink in.

"If there's one thing I don't like, it's a coincidence, so we aren't ruling out the possibility that the two incidents may turn out to be linked. However, let's not put the cart before the horse—we come to each investigation with an open mind, and consider each set of facts on their own merits. From an operational perspective, I will be the Senior Investigating Officer on the Tebbutt case, whilst DI

MacKenzie will be temporarily promoted to acting DCI, and will be the Senior Investigating Officer on the cathedral case."

He noticed a couple of junior officers lean forward in their seats to pat McKenzie's shoulder, by way of congratulations.

"I'm sure most of you will be aware that my wife was, and is, a material witness to what happened at the cathedral yesterday, as well as being a victim herself. That being the case, I want to assure all of you of my ongoing commitment to proper procedure throughout the running of these investigations."

He caught Morrison's eye, and gave the ghost of a smile.

"In my absence, Lowerson and Yates had the running of the crime scene yesterday, so I'll invite them to give us a summary of what we know so far."

Ryan leaned back against the desk at the front of the room, and gestured them both forward. It wasn't enough to solve crimes, or keep murderous degenerates off the streets. On a day-to-day level, it was his responsibility to ensure that the staff under his command were challenged and developed in line with their personal and professional goals. That included giving them a little nudge to practice skills that didn't come naturally, and, in the case of Jack Lowerson and Melanie Yates, neither particularly enjoyed public speaking.

But it came with the territory.

He watched a silent tussle between them, neither party willing to lead, until Yates eventually capitulated—but not before sending Lowerson a look that might have killed a lesser man.

"Um, well, what we know so far is that Joan Tebbutt had scrambled eggs on toast for breakfast, some tea and biscuits, and was probably looking forward to relaxing on her day off work,"

Yates said, with quiet authority. "Unfortunately, that wasn't meant to be. Four separate calls came in to the Control Room in Durham at around twelve-fifteen yesterday afternoon, each reporting gunshots fired on Albert Street, where Joan lived in Seaham. First responders were dispatched immediately, however no firearms officers were available to attend at that time, as they'd already been deployed to attend the incident in progress at the cathedral."

Yates paused to collect her thoughts before continuing.

"When first responding officers attended the scene, they found Joan straight away. Paramedics also attended but, as we now understand, Joan died almost immediately after suffering a fatal gunshot wound to the head."

"Had the body been touched?"

"Not to our knowledge," Yates replied. "None of her neighbours reported going near the body, because it was quite obvious that Joan had passed away. First responders checked the house for any signs of an intruder and checked Joan's pulse but, other than that, did not interfere with the scene. Following your instructions, Jack and myself were briefed at the earliest opportunity by the Chief Constable, and we made our way there as quickly as we could, arriving at around one-fifteen yesterday afternoon. CSIs had already been directed to protect the area, and representatives from Durham CID were…"

She paused, wondering how honest she should be.

"Let's say, they were loosely manning the scene."

Ryan's ears pricked up. "What do you mean?" he asked.

"I've put it all in my report," she said. "The fact is, we found the scene wide open, sir. Had it not been for the presence of Faulkner's team anybody might have been able to wander beneath the police line. I took the opportunity to…ah, remind the officers of their duties as regards crime scene security, and they assure me they won't make the same mistake again."

Lowerson sent her a sideways glance, and grinned.

"I'm glad to hear it," Ryan said. "Anything else?"

"We have informed her next of kin," Yates replied. "Joan leaves behind a daughter, who's making her way up from London."

Ryan nodded, understanding fully how difficult that conversation would have been, whilst acknowledging that it was another kind of skill she had now developed.

"Well done," he murmured.

"The pathologist has given his preliminary thoughts following post-mortem yesterday evening," Lowerson chipped in. "He's confirmed cause of death as a penetrating gunshot wound to the cranium."

Ryan folded his arms across his chest, the only outward indication of his anger and frustration at the waste of life.

"There were only two shots fired," Lowerson continued. "One missed the mark and grazed her neck, and the bullet was recovered from the front door by Faulkner's team. The second hit her, and was recovered by the pathologist. Both bullets have been sent to ballistics for testing, but they appear to be from the same firearm."

"What calibre?"

"Standard 9 mm," Lowerson replied.

"It takes a confident marksman to hit a target like that, using only two bullets," Ryan remarked. "What was the trajectory?"

"We completed house-to-house interviews today, and spoke with key witnesses yesterday afternoon," Yates said. "All four of Joan's neighbours who called in the incident witnessed a single person, wearing dark leathers and a dark helmet, escaping the scene on a motorbike. A couple more heard the motorbike but didn't see anything, and those who did see, can't say for certain whether this person was male or female, or give any other meaningful details about the rider's appearance. We've requested that they work with the police artist to try to build a better picture."

"Good," Ryan approved. "Go on."

"Presuming the motorcyclist is our assailant, it seems safe to assume that the shots were fired from the road. There's a distance of around twelve metres from where Joan fell in her doorway to some fresh tyre tracks found almost directly in front of Joan's house."

"Which suggests the rider paused to take the shots, then fled at speed, leaving rubber marks behind," Ryan said, visualising the scene. "Factoring in the distance, the weapon, and the limited window of time they had in which to fire a killing shot...we're looking for a serious marksman. A professional."

"Army, maybe?" Lowerson wondered.

"Or someone closer to home," Ryan said, darkly.

CHAPTER 16

As the sun fell lower in the sky and shone its last fiery rays over the city, it became clear to those in the police briefing that, despite Lowerson and Yates' best efforts, there were no leads in the Tebbutt case.

Faulkner's team of CSIs had spent the day picking over the minutiae of Joan's life, dusting every nook and cranny of her home for clues to her killer, without uncovering anything that could be described as suspicious. Work was ongoing, but there had been no smoking gun left conveniently on the pavement, nor any bloodied handprint on the garden gate. The pathologist could shed no further light on the matter, except to confirm the likely trajectory the bullet had taken before entering her skull, and to corroborate the reports from Joan's neighbours as to likely time of death. CCTV footage had been requested from any local businesses who boasted a camera, but the town of Seaham was a small one and there were a few establishments aside from pubs and clubs who bothered to spring for a sophisticated security system that would provide more than a flash of grainy footage. The Digital Forensics Team were in possession of Joan's mobile phone which, if they could unlock it, may shed some light on her recent movements and contacts. Likewise, they'd contacted Joan's landline telephone provider, though they already knew she'd spoken to her daughter on the morning she'd died.

In the meantime, Ryan had given orders that colleagues from Tebbutt's team at Durham CID should compile a full list of potential suspects who may have held a grudge against the dead woman. Admittedly, it could be a long list given her distinguished career, but the significant factor remained the timing—why kill Joan Tebbutt then, and not on another day?

"Separately, I want you to compile dossiers on each of the remaining members of Tebbutt's team, as well as all those she helped to remove," Ryan said. "Recall the files from Operation Watchman."

He did not relish the prospect of revisiting matters he'd thought were over and done with, but it was their task to shine a light into every dark corner.

"Get a list of recent releases, while you're at it," he added, thinking of the alerts they received when a prisoner was released— either on bail or because they'd served their time. It wasn't unheard of, for a criminal to bide their time before exacting revenge of a personal nature and, as Morrison had already observed, Tebbutt had been a target. "Cross-check against the firearms database, to see who has a license. I doubt the person we're looking for will have dutifully registered their weapon, but stranger things have happened."

He paused to check the clock on the wall.

Seven-twenty.

"I know time's marching on, so let's move on to the next item of business. Mac?"

He stepped away and, as a nod to his earlier commitment, took a seat on the front row alongside the rest of his team to allow MacKenzie to lead the second half of the briefing.

* * *

For her part, McKenzie had led too many briefings to count, but never one where her moniker was, 'Detective Chief Inspector'. Before Samantha had come into their lives, she might have sought a more permanent promotion but, seeing how hard Ryan worked—not only on active cases, but in supervising the running of all the cases in his division, on top of the usual bureaucracy and other tedious administrative tasks he was required to perform— had given her pause for thought. She may never have harboured longstanding dreams of becoming a mother but, to her surprise, it had come very naturally. More importantly, she enjoyed Samantha's company, and liked having a separation between work and home that afforded her time enough in the day to spend it with her little girl.

Yet, standing at the head of the conference room, her old ambition reared its head again as she realised that this, too, came very naturally. She could easily imagine running her own division, and was undaunted by the prospect of dealing with a greater share of police politics or running a high-profile case, such as the one she had now been tasked to lead.

At that moment, it was as if the universe had heard the voice inside her head, for it chose to remind her of the physical impediment she now suffered and which often prevented her from leading as busy and active life as she once had. A stab of referred pain reverberated through her leg and she might have buckled, had she not been so aware of the eyes that watched and waited expectantly for her to begin her part of the briefing.

Conscious not to let the weakness show, McKenzie leaned back against the desk as Ryan had done a short while before.

"You should see in your packs a summary document I created earlier today, following a handover briefing with DCI Ryan," she said, and was proud of how normal she managed to sound. "My thanks to him for his detailed records of the case so far, which I'll summarise for you now."

She made a show of reaching for her file, to buy herself a few moments' respite.

"Firstly, let's recap the facts," she said. "Shortly after noon yesterday, person or persons unknown detonated what we now know to have been four smoke bombs. Witness accounts tell us that these bombs were detonated simultaneously, causing very loud explosions and emitting a large quantity of smoke into the central areas of the cathedral. Structural engineers have confirmed the cathedral remains fully intact and undamaged, which, taken together with the fact that Saint Cuthbert's cross was stolen from its display cabinet in the Great Kitchen sometime during the chaos, would suggest that the primary purpose of these bombs was to disrupt and disorientate—thereby facilitating the robbery in progress."

She paused to allow the team to flip over the next page of their packs, while she rubbed a surreptitious hand over her bad leg.

"We also know that the perpetrators of this crime were not averse to using violence, and we see this from the serious injuries sustained by Dr Anna Taylor-Ryan."

At the mention of her name, Ryan couldn't prevent the quick flare of anger and concern, but he reminded himself that she was in the best possible hands and would, all being well, return home the next day.

"There were three others who sustained minor injuries as they scrambled to escape what they believed to be a terror attack," McKenzie continued. "Each of those individuals has been interviewed by colleagues from Durham CID, but none of them witnessed anything or anyone that would provide us with a useful lead. Doctor Taylor-Ryan remains our primary potential witness—however, she sustained a serious head injury during the attack, which has precipitated some short-term memory loss. I know that DCI Ryan will be able to update us with any developments on that score, however our primary concern is that Doctor Taylor-Ryan should continue to recover at her own pace, without undue stress or interference from us."

Ryan sent her a grateful smile, which she returned.

"Our working hypothesis is that Doctor Taylor-Ryan was attacked by the same person, or persons, who managed to gain entry to the display case which held St Cuthbert's cross. It is our belief that, unfortunately, she found herself very much in the wrong place at the wrong time."

It disturbed McKenzie to think of her friend in such peril, but she thrust the thought from her mind. Like Ryan, she knew that it did no good to dwell on the things she couldn't change; instead, she redirected her emotion towards the things she *could*.

"The smoke bombs are presently with the bomb squad for further analysis," she continued. "It's possible we may be able to trace some of their component parts. However, at the moment what we know for sure is that their primary purpose was to set off the fire alarm and cause widespread panic. That will be our starting point."

"Do we know how these devices were planted?" Morrison asked. "Durham Cathedral is a major tourist spot, so it seems remarkable that they made it inside the building at all."

"I've been liaising with our colleagues at Durham CID—DS Carter and DC Winter—and I understand there are no restrictions on bags coming into the cathedral itself; only the Exhibition Galleries. That being the case, it would have been easy to plant three of the devices, which were found in the nave of the cathedral, but harder to plant the device that was discovered in the Great Kitchen, which is where the robbery took place."

She lifted a shoulder.

"At this point, ma'am, we're still investigating how that device got through the security barriers and into the exhibition space, but we've received the first batch of CCTV footage from the cathedral's head of security, and we'll be analysing that as a priority in the coming days."

Morrison nodded, and MacKenzie took that as a signal to continue.

"As for the robbery, the only damage was to the display case itself, which was made of reinforced, high-density polymer. It was designed to be unbreakable without specialist equipment, and we understand from the Cathedral's Chief Operating Officer that all of the display cases in the area were re-fitted following major renovation works three years ago."

"I've seen *YouTube* videos about this," Lowerson said. "Those things really are unbreakable—how the hell did they manage to get into it?"

"With something as simple as an axe," McKenzie replied. "If they'd used a battering ram or a bullet, they would hardly have made a dent in the polymer, but with the right kind of finely-honed edge, a few good whacks are all it takes to weaken and eventually splinter the facing."

"Where have I heard about this happening before?" Yates wondered aloud.

"There was a similar incident last year in Germany," Ryan said. "Robbers made off with jewels worth hundreds of millions of pounds from a museum in Dresden after smashing a similar security case using an axe."

This was news to McKenzie, who made a hasty note to look it up.

"What was the outcome in that case?" she asked him.

"Nothing was ever recovered," he replied, ominously. "The robbers and the jewels are still at large."

"This throws up a whole new line of enquiry," Morrison said. "What if it was the same gang operating in Durham as in Dresden?"

"It's possible," Ryan mused. "But, in the case of Dresden, they hit a museum and stole several items in bulk. Here, you have one very specific artefact."

"Which is made of pure gold, and garnet," Morrison reminded him.

There was a short silence, until McKenzie broke it.

"If it is the same gang, they've just bitten off a lot more than they can chew," she said, with quiet determination. "I'll contact the German police first thing tomorrow morning to see if there's anything more they can tell us but, on the face of it, we have to generate our own leads. So far, no equipment has been recovered, nor the implement used to attack Doctor Taylor-Ryan. Interviews with the staff and volunteers of the cathedral are ongoing, but I have a feeling that whatever we are looking for will be like finding a needle in a haystack."

"What can we do?" Ryan asked.

MacKenzie looked him in the eye.

"Ryan, I know you'll be focusing most of your attention on the Tebbutt case," she said, by way of friendly reminder. "If you find any crossover between the two incidents, I know you'll inform us straight away. As far as possible, and for obvious reasons, I will be seeking to keep the two investigations separate. That includes my working relationship with the staff at Durham CID, who have so far been very accommodating—but we don't know how long that will last, once things started to heat up in Tebbutt's murder. In the meantime, if Anna is able to remember any pertinent facts following her attack, we'd like to know. Otherwise, if she's in a position to advise us of any reason why Cuthbert's cross would be of particular value to a certain type of criminal than any of the other artefacts, then her professional expertise would be extremely valuable."

Ryan had to agree that Anna would be perfectly placed to consult on the historic background to the artefact that had been stolen. In their world, they often looked to the victim for clues about their attacker, and there was no reason why it should be any different in the case of a violent robbery—in other words, they should look to Cuthbert's cross to understand its importance in the eyes of the person who took it.

"Lowerson," McKenzie was saying. "I'd like you to accompany me tomorrow when I make a visit to the cathedral, and then to our colleagues in Durham CID. Yates, if you could act as reader-receiver over the course of the investigation, that would be greatly appreciated given the volume of statements and other data we'll need to manage."

"Consider it done," Yates said.

"Separately, I'd like all of us to consider known gangs or individuals with previous form for this type of aggravated high-end robbery. We'll contact national, European, and other international enforcement agencies to compile a list."

While MacKenzie continued to set out her instructions for the running of the investigation, the sky outside turned a fiery shade of red as day turned into night.

"Tomorrow is a new day," McKenzie told them. "Go home now and get plenty of rest—tomorrow, the battle begins again."

But, as the others began to file out, Ryan lingered for a moment to speak with his friend.

"You're a natural leader," he said. "You inspired confidence back there, which is no easy task when your audience is a room full of cynical murder detectives."

She chuckled.

"Tough crowd," she agreed.

"Well, you made it look easy," he said. "Look, we've talked about this before, but I'll say it again: are you sure you don't want to make this promotion a more permanent fixture?"

McKenzie sighed, wondering how to answer.

"I'd love nothing more than to take you up on that offer," she said. "If I'd been the same woman I was three years ago, I'd be biting your hand off…but, I'm not the same woman, Ryan. I've changed, and I can't go back to being the person I was before. Even now, I struggle to stand on this bloody leg for longer than a few minutes at a time, so how could I cope with more travel, more responsibilities?"

Ryan had seen her go pale at the start of the meeting and had put it down to nerves. Now he knew the real reason, he wished he'd been right.

"Mac, you never really talk about it—"

"Pride, I suppose," she said. "Silly, isn't it?"

"No, it's not silly," he replied. "What about a physiotherapist?"

She smiled, grateful to have a friend who wanted to help her, however he could. But Ryan was no Superman, nor did he have a magic wand.

"I see a physio twice a week, as I have for the past three years, but it's the scar tissue. It's tightened around my muscle and keeps getting worse."

"Can't you have an operation to remove it?" he asked. "Why not get a second opinion?"

And a third and a fourth, she thought, with a smile.

"I'm a very lucky woman," she said. "I have my life, I have Frank and a lovely little girl, and a job that makes me happy. It would be greedy to wish for more."

Ryan simply shook its head.

"We can find a way," he said, stubbornly. "You shouldn't be held back by anything."

There it was, McKenzie thought. His unshakeable belief that he could make the world better, and that there was always something worth fighting for, was the reason he was so admired, even by those who feared him.

She leaned in to kiss his cheek.

"Thank you," she said quietly. "I'll keep it in mind."

The conversation was closed as far as she was concerned, but as she walked slowly and carefully from the room, Ryan was left with the germ of an idea.

It would keep.

CHAPTER 17

Ryan and Anna had chosen to build their home in an idyllic corner of the world, resting at the top of a gentle hillside overlooking the ancient village of Elsdon. It held panoramic views of the Northumbrian countryside and, on a clear day, they could see for miles in any direction.

It was a place of big skies, and big dreams.

But, as he drove back from the city, Ryan couldn't muster any of the joy he usually felt at the prospect of going home; not when every passing mile took him further away from the woman he loved. Only now that she had come through the worst of it did his mind allow him to truly comprehend what it would have meant to lose her, and the beauty of a starry night sky was not enough to salve the pain of what might have been.

Consumed by thoughts of how to find the person responsible, Ryan almost forgot about the visitors who awaited his return. A shiny Land Rover was parked on the gravel driveway, its tinted windows and nondescript license plate both subtle reminders of its owner's pedigree. Charles Ryan was an important man, who'd given everything to Queen and Country for all of his sixty-seven years, leaving little for the family who'd lovingly waited for him at home—and, my, what a home it had been. Ryan had been born in a stately pile in Devonshire, which his father had inherited from *his* father, who'd inherited it from *his* father before him.

Lovely bricks and mortar, like the cathedral, Ryan thought. And just as cold.

Ryan turned off the engine of his own car and sat there until the cool night air began to seep inside, chilling the hands he rested limply in his lap.

He hardly noticed the cold, lingering there in the silent car, his mind awash with swirling memories of the past.

Daddy? Will you play with me?

I'm busy, Maxwell. Go and find a useful occupation, for heaven's sake.

Angry with himself, angry with the child he had been, Ryan slammed out of the car and crunched across the gravel towards the front door. He was no longer a child, eager and desperate to please a man too important to find the time to play games. It hadn't mattered then, and it didn't matter now.

He schooled his features into a neutral mask before opening the door.

Whatever he'd been expecting, it wasn't the warm, exotic scent of mixed spices wafting down the hallway from the kitchen, nor the sound of mellow jazz from the radio. Ryan's stomach gave a loud rumble, reminding him that it had been a considerable time since he'd last eaten.

Still, he took his time hanging up his jacket and toeing off his boots, setting them beside Anna's trainers, which stood neatly on the rack.

He couldn't say why the sight of them was enough to bring tears to his eyes.

"There you are! I was beginning to worry."

His mother's quick footsteps sounded along the flagstone hallway and he found himself enveloped in his second maternal hug of the day. He worried that he'd grow used to them, and it would be all the harder to say goodbye when she inevitably left.

Just like before.

"I had a briefing," he said, gently peeling her away. "Something smells good."

Eve swallowed the immediate sense of rejection, and pinned a smile on her face.

"It's homemade Thai curry," she said. "It used to be your favourite, when you were little."

Ryan barely stopped himself making a caustic remark about her not knowing what his likes and dislikes were, considering he'd spent the majority of his time at an expensive boarding school from the age of seven. The strength of his own resentment surprised him, and he put it down to being over-tired and stressed.

"How was Anna, when you left her?" he asked instead.

"Oh, looking so much better," Eve said. "They say she should be able to come home in the morning. We can collect her, if you like?"

"No, thank you," he said, with rigid politeness. "I want to be there, myself."

Eve nodded, and led the way into the kitchen.

"You've made a lovely home here," she said, gesturing to the pictures on the walls, and the pretty keepsakes they'd collected on their travels.

"That's mostly Anna," he said. "She has an eye for things like that."

"It takes two, to build a home," his mother replied.

Ryan said nothing, but his eyes slid over to the conservatory area, where his father had installed himself in an armchair with a book about local history—probably one of Anna's.

"Have you eaten?" his mother asked. "We thought we'd wait for you."

He was surprised.

"There was no need to wait," he said. "You must be exhausted from your drive."

Eve said nothing, but thought privately that she didn't feel half as exhausted as her son looked.

"It's been a very worrying time for you," she said softly, reaching out again to take his hand. "Please, let me help."

There was a pleading in her voice, a yearning he couldn't ignore, and Ryan simply nodded.

"When Anna comes home from the hospital—"

"Of course, we'll be here for her," Eve said. "She's a wonderful girl, and you know I've always thought very highly of her. But I'm worried about you, too. You seem…"

Ryan raised an eyebrow.

"How do I seem?"

"Angry," she said, and let her hand fall away.

Ryan moved away to pace around the kitchen, which felt stifling and small, all of a sudden. Now was not the time to tell her that thoughts of impending fatherhood had caused him to rake over his own childhood, and to wish that they'd been poor, or less 'important' so that he could have grown up without ever doubting his parents' love. Now was not the time to tell her of the long nights he'd cried in his dormitory bunk as a small boy, wondering why his mother and father had left him, wondering why they didn't want to be with him. She wouldn't want to know how much it had affected him—would she ever want to know how hard it had been for him to trust people, or to learn how to form lasting relationships, until he'd met Anna?

Yes, he was angry.

It was decades-old and unresolved; a wound that continued to weep, no matter how he tried to plaster over it, or find remedies for the pain. Now, they'd come to help him, and he wanted to be grateful; but he'd needed the help thirty years before, as the child he'd been, and it was a little late now.

But it was not the time to say any of that.

"I'll set the table," was all he said.

* * *

Dinner was a quiet affair, and everybody retired to bed soon afterwards.

Ryan was restless without Anna by his side, his body tossing and turning as disjointed half-dreams of nightmarish explosions drove him from sleep. Eventually, he gave up on the prospect altogether, and padded back downstairs shortly before dawn.

But he was not the only one who had been unable to sleep.

He found his father standing by the window in the kitchen-diner, already fully dressed for the day. It was a position Ryan often occupied, and he experienced a funny jolt of recognition because, just for a moment, it was as though he was looking upon his future self.

Charles turned, breaking the odd little daydream.

"You're up early," he said. "There's coffee in the pot."

It was one of the few things they had in common, Ryan thought. Aside from their physical attributes, both men had a weakness for strong coffee.

"Lovely view from the window here," his father continued, while Ryan poured them each a fresh cup. "Your mother tells me you chose the spot yourself?"

Ryan was disoriented by his father's easy, conversational manner; he had very little experience of it.

"Yes," he said. "The land was a wedding present to Anna. We designed the house ourselves, and had it built so we could look out across the hills."

"You always did like to be outdoors," his father said, taking a sip of the coffee Ryan offered him. "I never thought you'd stay in London."

"I enjoyed it for a time," Ryan said, casting his mind back to when he'd first moved to the capital as a young man. He'd done his time at Police College and taken up his first post at the Met—which had been an education, in more ways than one.

But his father was right.

A yearning for rugged landscapes and unpredictable weather had lured him north, where he'd found his true place in the world.

"Are you happy in Devon?"

It was a beautiful county, Ryan thought, and there was much to admire. But that wasn't necessarily the same thing as feeling at home, and he wondered if his father had ever found his 'place' in the world.

Charles seemed baffled by the question.

"Happy?" He gave a negligent shrug. "I—well, it's where I grew up. Summerley Park has been in the family for generations, so there was never really any choice in the matter."

There was always a choice, Ryan thought, and looked down at the mug he held in his hand. It happened to display a faded motif of himself and Phillips, their faces superimposed onto the cartoon bodies of Batman and Robin. He smiled, and another question entered his mind—one he hadn't really considered before.

"Do you have friends there?" Ryan asked. "I don't mean people you have to socialise with. I mean people you can laugh with, and be yourself with."

Charles stared out at the undulating landscape, watching it slowly come alive in the first rays of morning.

"I have your mother," he said. "She's been my best friend for over forty years. She understands me, as Anna understands you. That's more than many could boast."

In that simple, powerful statement, Ryan realised that he and his father had another thing in common: they each had been blessed with the love of a better person than themselves.

They stood in companionable silence until Ryan set his mug back down on the counter.

"I should get on with some work," he said. "There's a lot to do, today."

Charles nodded, understanding only too well. Then, his eye fell upon a small chess set made from carved marble. It belonged to Anna, who had brought it back from a holiday in Egypt, but now it sat on a bookshelf gathering dust.

Ryan turned to leave, but his father's voice stopped him.

"I wonder…that is, I wondered if you'd like to play? Do you have the time?"

He pointed to the chess set.

Ryan stared at it, and then him, for long seconds.

How many times had he wished to hear those words?

How often had he uttered them himself?

But here was an olive branch, and Ryan could choose whether to grasp it or not.

Dawn sunlight burned brightly through the polished windowpanes, illuminating the two men who faced one another in the silent morning.

"Yes," Ryan said, hoarsely. "I'd like that very much."

CHAPTER 18

"I think I could walk home faster than this!"

Ryan had collected Anna from the hospital as soon as its doors opened. Since then, he'd treated her as though she was made of finely-cut glass, liable to break at the slightest touch. Whilst it was true that her body had been through a traumatic ordeal, Anna could feel her strength returning by the hour and she had no wish to be treated like anybody's maiden aunt.

Or to be driven around the countryside like *Miss Daisy*, for that matter.

"Better safe than sorry," Ryan said. "There are a lot of idiots on the road."

Anna held off remarking that, by driving as slowly as he was, some might say *he* was the aforementioned idiot. However, she knew how worried Ryan had been, and so held her tongue and resigned herself to a leisurely journey home.

"How are you feeling?" he asked, for the fiftieth time that hour.

"Just the same as I was before," she replied. "Stiff and sore, but ready to re-enter the land of the living."

Ryan knew it was more than a little soreness, and checked the dashboard clock to see when she was allowed her next dose of pain relief. At least her speech had improved, which the doctors told him was an excellent sign.

"How's the baby?" he asked, to take her mind off things.

"She's full of beans, this morning," Anna said, and then sent him a startled glance. "I wonder why I keep thinking of the baby as a girl."

"Perhaps, because she *is* a girl," he said softly.

Anna closed her eyes, trying to snatch at the thread of a memory which floated to the surface of her mind.

"Did—did you tell me that before?"

"I spoke to you about it while you were sleeping. The surgeon told me the sex of the baby by accident, and I thought it was unfair to keep you in the dark."

He glanced across at her.

"Did I do the right thing?

Anna smiled, the pain in her head forgotten.

"Yes, you did the right thing," she said, rubbing absent circles over her belly.

A girl.

"I was so scared we'd lose her," she murmured. "I wish I could remember what happened, so I can help you try to find who did this."

"It'll come back to you," Ryan said.

And, even if it doesn't, I'll still find the bastard responsible, he added silently.

Anna stared out at the passing scenery, one hand pressed to her temple as she tried to remember.

"It's no good," she said, frustrated with herself. "I just keep seeing the cross hanging there in its case, all shiny and golden, then the smoke and the explosions, and people screaming. There's a crash, and then nothing."

"A crash?" Ryan queried.

She nodded.

"Yes, I'm almost certain there was a kind of loud crashing or cracking sound. Didn't I mention that before?"

"No, that's new, so it must have just come back to you," he said, with an encouraging smile.

"Still, it doesn't help much, does it?" she said. "I wish there was something more I could do—I feel like a big, useless lump."

"Don't say that," he said. "You're looking after our baby, and you don't have a useless bone in your body. In fact, there may be something you can help us with, if you're feeling up to it."

She turned to him with curious brown eyes.

"What is it?"

"Some historical expertise," he replied. "You already know that the explosions at the cathedral caused no real damage to the building. It seems their entire purpose was to cause a diversion while Cuthbert's cross was stolen."

Anna nodded.

"It's been all over the news."

"I understand that the cross is made of gold, but I'm more inclined to think its value lies in its historical significance, rather than its materials," Ryan said. "Would you agree?"

"Yes, definitely. It's the cultural significance that makes it irreplaceable."

Ryan nodded.

"We think some kind of small axe or other implement was used to break into the polymer display casing," he explained. The information was, after all, something that might easily be ascertained in the public domain. "There was a major robbery in Dresden last year, where thieves made off with jewellery worth hundreds of millions. They managed to break into the same kind of high-spec display casing, without ever being caught."

"You think the same thieves who stole the jewellery in Dresden may now have taken Cuthbert's cross?"

"We have to explore the possibility," Ryan said. "But, in the Dresden case, the jewellery could be broken down and sold in bulk. It isn't the same here."

Anna could see his predicament.

"If somebody stole the cross to order, then it was probably all arranged on the black market," she said. "How will you ever trace it?"

Ryan flicked the indicator to come off the dual carriageway.

"There are ways and means," he said. "But it's a long and difficult process, with only a small chance of success—which is why I'm coming at it from the other direction. To understand who might want it, and try to build up a picture of a perpetrator who may already be known to us, I need to know: why *that* cross, in particular? Why not any of the other pieces on display at the cathedral, or at any of the other museums around the country?"

"It's small, so could be easily transported," she thought aloud. "But there are other small pieces they might have taken from other museums and stately homes, so it's safe to assume the local connection was important. To cause such a commotion and go to such lengths to create the optimal conditions to take it, I doubt the size or weight of the artefact was too much of a factor in the decision-making process."

Ryan agreed.

"I think whoever did this had an order to fulfil, and they would have formulated a plan regardless of the artefact they'd been asked to take."

They were silent for a moment, each considering the kind of person who could plan and execute such a heist.

"It's a beautiful cross," Anna mused. "But there are other beautiful items from that time period. If the significance relates to Cuthbert, rather than to the cross itself, then that's a more interesting question."

Ryan realised that, although he'd heard the name of the saint bandied around, he actually knew very little about the man himself, or how he'd risen to prominence.

"I know that Cuthbert was a monk at the priory on Lindisfarne," he said, and thought how strange it was that so many strands of their life seemed entwined with that little holy island. It was where Anna had been born and where, years later, they had met during the course of a murder investigation.

He imagined things were different, back in Cuthbert's day.

"Can you give me a kind of executive summary?" he asked.

"How much can you handle?" she asked, with a chuckle. "I could talk for hours about early religious history in these parts."

"I've missed hearing your voice," he said, quietly. "You can talk to me all day about anything you want, but it might as well be Cuthbert, since it'll help the case."

Anna pressed a kiss to her fingertips, then reached across with her good arm to brush it against his lips.

"Charmer," she said.

"I've been taking lessons from Frank." He grinned.

"He's a good teacher," she agreed, and then settled in for a chat about one of her favourite topics. "Let's see. Well, growing up on Holy Island, it was hard to escape the Cuthbert connection, even if I'd wanted to. He was actually born in Dunbar in the mid-630s AD, which is part of Scotland now but, back then, was part of Anglo-Saxon Northumbria. The area had converted to Christianity just before he was born, but it was going through a violent transition around that time, interspersed with episodes of pagan rule."

"It can still be a source of disagreement," Ryan muttered.

"Around the same time Cuthbert was born, the king at the time, Oswald, invited monks over from Iona to establish a monastery at Lindisfarne."

"I remember Oswald," Ryan said. "Not personally, of course," he added, to make her laugh.

Anna nodded, and was relieved that her ramblings about local history hadn't fallen entirely on deaf ears.

"He was one of the first kings of England, and very powerful at the time. Getting back to Cuthbert, he was essentially a travelling missionary, who tried to spread the Christian message to remote villages around the kingdom. Apparently, he was very adept with royalty and nobility, as well as being able to converse with everyday people, which made him very popular. For all that, he lived the life of a hermit whenever he could, receiving the odd visitor when he felt like it."

"Sounds blissful," Ryan said.

"You'd miss people more than you think," Anna said. "Cuthbert had a reputation for miracles and healing. He carried on being a missionary for most of his career, even after he was made Prior of the Monastery at Melrose. Then, around 676 AD, he took himself off to what's now known as 'Saint Cuthbert's Cave', near Holburn."

"That's not far from us," Ryan said. "I've been meaning to go."

"I'm surprised a dead body hasn't turned up inside there," Anna remarked. "Seems a good spot for it."

"Too obvious," Ryan said simply, and braked gently so as not to jolt her neck.

"Yes, I suppose the cave is on the pilgrimage trail," Anna said. "Hundreds of people walk the trail each year, following in Cuthbert's footsteps all the way to the island. A killer wouldn't have too much privacy, with all those pilgrims stomping about."

Ryan looked across at her with shining eyes.

"Every time, I'm amazed at how bloodthirsty you are," he said. "And you, a quiet historian."

"It's always the quiet ones," she reminded him.

"True. What did Cuthbert do after he'd finished being a hermit in his cave?"

"He moved to the island of Inner Farne, to be a hermit there," she said.

"Too many wolves around the caves, I expect," Ryan said, with the flash of a smile.

"Life on Inner Farne wouldn't have been much better," she said. "It's tiny, hardly more than an oversized rock, and completely open to the elements. You know what the weather can be like, in the Farne Islands."

They both did, especially after a recent investigation that had taken them on a journey of exploration in the Farnes, to the graveyard of shipwrecks far below the murky waterline. The coastline in the North East was treacherous, and Mother Nature could be merciless to those who ventured out in a storm.

"Cuthbert built a tiny cell for himself, and stayed there," Anna said. "He kept mostly to himself, only receiving visitors very rarely. The records say one of the few interviews he granted was to the Holy Abbess and Royal Virgin, Elfleda—"

"*Elf-leader?*" Ryan repeated, and was struck by a terrible thought. "Promise me, you're not thinking of calling our daughter some old Anglo-Saxon name like that?"

Anna wriggled her eyebrows.

"Elfleda was the daughter of Oswiu, who succeeded Hilda as abbess of Whitby in 680," she said. "You know, *Hilda Taylor-Ryan* has a certain… ring to it," she said.

Ryan sent her a panicked look, wondering what the parenting manuals said about moments such as these. He followed the turn for Elsdon and told himself there was still plenty of time to talk her out of any rash decision-making.

"What happened after he was visited by the, ah, royal virgin?" he asked. "Or would it be impolite to ask?"

Anna laughed.

"You'd be surprised how many crazy theories there are about Cuthbert's legacy," she said. "Anyway, he was elected Bishop of

Hexham in 684 AD, but didn't want to take up his post and leave his life as a hermit."

"All the cold weather must have sent him off his chump," Ryan said, and she laughed again.

"You'll be glad to know, they managed to talk Cuthbert around, on condition he could return to monastic life and take up the duties as Bishop of Lindisfarne, instead of Hexham. As it turned out, he wasn't in the post very long before he went back to his little cell on Inner Farne, which is where he died on 20th March 687 AD, only three years after he was made bishop."

"Seems fitting he died in the place he loved," Ryan remarked. He knew better than most that it didn't always happen that way. He thought again of Joan Tebbutt, and took some comfort in the knowledge she had died quickly, and at home.

"There's a shrine at Durham Cathedral to Cuthbert, and his remains are buried underneath the stones there," he said. "How did he end up all the way down in Durham, if he died on Lindisfarne?"

It was over an hour's drive in a modern car, on clear roads, so it would have been a considerably longer journey back in the seventh century.

"Cuthbert was buried at Lindisfarne on the same day he died, but his remains didn't stay there—the monks carried his body over hill and vale, to escape the Danes. There is a trail to show the journey his remains took before eventually settling in Durham."

"So, even back then, he was important enough to protect—even in death?" Ryan asked.

Anna nodded.

"Bringing him to Durham was the catalyst for the foundation of the city and Durham Cathedral. Cuthbert—or, rather, his remains—were responsible for the city as we know it."

Ryan wound the car through Elsdon, and slowed to a crawl to allow one of their neighbours to stick their head through the window and wish Anna a speedy recovery.

Once they'd waved her off again, the conversation continued.

"I'm trying to put myself into the shoes of someone who'd want to take that cross," Anna said. "Lindisfarne is important from a historical perspective because it was the site of one of the earliest recorded Viking raids on the United Kingdom. It has religious significance because of its strong Christian history, and it has literary significance, too. The Gospels were written there, after all."

"But if they'd wanted to steal something of literary value, they could have taken either of the two copies of the Magna Carta which are held at the library, right there on Palace Green," Ryan pointed out.

"Or they could have taken St Cuthbert's Gospel," Anna said. "It's the earliest known example of a bound book, and was buried with Cuthbert shortly after his death. It's also held in the Cathedral, so it would have been easy enough to take that, instead."

Ryan accelerated as they climbed towards the top of the hill.

"It has to be someone local or with strong ties to the region," he decided. "Or else, a collector with a particular interest in monastic history, specifically Cuthbert."

Anna yawned, feeling tired all of a sudden.

"If this Cuthbert was such a humble man, why did he have such a flashy cross?" Ryan asked. "Surely, that would have been worth a pretty penny, even back then."

Anna smiled.

"He may be a saint now, but he was only a man then," she replied. "He was a good man, by all accounts, but that didn't mean he was oblivious to all that glitters."

"I wonder if there were other things he wasn't oblivious to," Ryan said.

"Historians are discovering new things all the time," Anna said. "We analyse clues to the past and formulate theories about what they might mean. There are probably countless treasures, not all of them made of gold, that we haven't found yet."

Ryan brought the car to a standstill, pleased to have made it home with his precious cargo still in one piece.

"I can understand your love of the past, and your desire to study objects which represent our shared history," he said. "I can't understand why any one person alone would covet something that should, by rights, belong to all the world."

Anna reached across to run a hand over the stubble on his cheek.

"You forgot to shave," she said. "You don't understand it, because you've never coveted anything. You didn't have to."

Ryan thought of all the children who'd grown up at home with their families, living a normal life, where their parents didn't delegate their job to bodyguards or nannies.

"Didn't I?" he asked, with an enigmatic smile. "If I ever did, I don't have to anymore."

He turned his face to kiss the underside of her palm.

"Welcome home, my love."

CHAPTER 19

The Headquarters of Durham Police Constabulary were based on a large site in Consett, a small town to the west of the city, where Joan Tebbutt had spent much of her working life. Like many government-owned buildings, it was unlikely to win any architectural awards for its general aesthetic, but its functional space was designed to inspire hard graft, not oil paintings.

Although a much-depleted unit, the Major Crimes Team was still required to assist MacKenzie with her investigation into the robbery and attack on Durham Cathedral. Amid all the work surrounding that incident, Tebbutt's staff barely had an opportunity to come to terms with their loss. It therefore came as something of a shock when Ryan and Phillips presented themselves in the foyer of the building, like distant cousins from another branch of the same large and unwieldy family, whom they'd rather only see once or twice a year.

"Feels funny, doesn't it?" Philip said, under his breath.

"I wouldn't like to comment on your prostate," Ryan shot back.

"Har bloody har," Phillips replied. "It'll be your face that looks funny, if you keep on crackin' jokes like that. I'm saying, it feels *funny*—being here, rather than over on our own turf."

Ryan nodded, watching a young constable pass by with a wide, gaping look on his face.

"That one should be careful he doesn't catch flies, walking around with his mouth hanging open like that," Phillips said. "I keep tellin' myself, we're only here to interview the people who knew Joan, just like we would in any murder investigation, but the fact is—"

"I know," Ryan muttered. "The fact is, one of them might be involved."

They watched people coming and going, including the police staff who buzzed themselves through a security door to access the executive suite beyond. It was a similar set-up to their own headquarters back in the east end of Newcastle, even down to the dubious clientele.

Speaking of which, at that very moment, a woman was escorted into the building by two constables, hissing and spitting about being manhandled. Her skinny legs were bare and unwashed, and she showed signs of extensive drug abuse.

"We've told you before, Sue. There are charities that can help you—"

"I don't want any bloody do-gooder comin' around tellin' me what I should and shouldn't do, and all that. I just want to go home. Why won't you let me go *home*?"

But she wouldn't go home, Ryan thought. She'd go straight back on the streets, to earn enough money to score her next high. Addiction was a cruel and vicious cycle, often leading to disease or death, either by their own persistent hand or by somebody else's.

Either way, he and Phillips were often the ones to look after them, in the end.

"DCI Ryan? DS Phillips? Good to see you, again."

They turned to find DS Ben Carter approaching them, his shoes squeaking across the tiled floor. Their first thought was that he seemed younger here than he had appeared beneath the dim lights of the cathedral. Yet there was a quality to the man that was ageless—whether it was the conservative haircut, his generic blue suit or general demeanour, they couldn't say; but it was easy to see how the young man had been promoted so quickly. He had a dependable, dogmatic quality to his personality which was well suited to the life they led.

"I spoke with DCI MacKenzie earlier," Carter said, as they made their way along the corridors towards Major Crimes. "She rang to introduce herself. I hope you won't mind me saying DS Phillips, but you're a very fortunate man."

"Don't mind at all, son," Philips said, good-naturedly. "Since it's nothing but the truth, and none who knows it better than me."

Carter smiled.

"I understand DCI MacKenzie will be handling the investigation into the robbery at the cathedral, and you'll be leading the investigation into DCI Tebbutt's murder," Carter said to Ryan. "That being the case, sir, I'd like to say that we all thought very highly of Joan, and you won't find any obstruction from our end. We all feel that, if it had to be anyone outside of our area command to handle her case, we're glad it's you."

"That's much appreciated," Ryan said, and hoped it was true. "I didn't know Joan well, but I knew her well enough to respect her skills as a detective and her integrity as a person."

A flicker of sadness passed over Carter's clean-shaven face.

"We were all stunned by the news," he said. "First, the cathedral, then this…I think it's only just beginning to sink in."

"It'll mean more responsibility for you," Phillips said, watching him closely.

"I suppose you're right. Here's the office."

They entered what might, ordinarily, be a bustling open-plan division, now sadly bereft of personnel. A few officers were seated around the room, and looked up as they entered.

"No DC Winter today?" Phillips asked.

Carter shook his head.

"Justine only works part-time," he told them. "She looks after her disabled brother two days a week."

"What about the rest?" Ryan asked.

"You're looking at them," Carter said, with a resigned shrug. "We've got a few out in the field interviewing staff and volunteers at the cathedral but, as you know, we lost a good number of senior staff members following Operation Watchman."

Ryan made a noncommittal sound in the back of his throat.

"Was this Tebbutt's desk?" he asked, pointing towards the one he would have chosen.

"Yeah, how did you know?"

"You can see the whole room from here," he said, and moved along the aisle towards her cubicle, so he could try to visualise the woman in her day-to-day life.

"We'll need access to her e-mail server," he said, and Carter nodded.

"Do you know where she kept the key for this?"

Ryan tapped a locked drawer at the bottom of Tebbutt's desk, but Carter shook his head.

"It's probably on her keyring or somewhere at home," he said. "You gave instructions that nothing should be removed from her house, so we haven't altered anything at the address, sir."

Usually, Ryan would not stand on ceremony. He preferred to be addressed by his name rather than his title but, given the circumstances, he didn't say anything.

"I'll send over one of our specialists from Digital Forensics," he said. "They'll need to go through her hard drive."

"Don't you want me to contact the Digital Forensics team here?"

Ryan took the opportunity to draw a firm line in the sand.

"No, we'll be outsourcing everything to Northumbria. I know this won't be easy, Carter. Our work will feel invasive and, at times, you might feel offended. I won't apologise for that, because it comes with the territory and you should know that it's my job to make sure Joan receives a fully-independent eye. That can't happen unless we take everything off-site, right down to the service personnel we use."

The broader ramifications of what Ryan was saying, as well is all he was *not* saying, seemed finally to hit home.

"Of course," Carter said, stiffly. "We'll accommodate whichever digital forensics specialist you choose, sir."

"Good," Ryan said. "Now, shall we find somewhere to sit and take down your statement?"

"I've already given a statement to Lowerson and Yates."

"So you did," Ryan said. "But I have a terrible habit of wanting to hear things from the horse's mouth."

On which note, he set off in search of an empty meeting room and a vending machine, because he had just realised it had been more than two hours since his last caffeine hit.

A man couldn't be expected to work in those conditions.

CHAPTER 20

While Ryan raided the vending machine at Durham Constabulary Headquarters, MacKenzie and Lowerson made their way through the crowded streets of the city, a few miles further east. While forensic work was still ongoing inside the cathedral, MacKenzie had agreed to remove the police cordon to allow pedestrian traffic to resume around Palace Green. However, there was no time to stop and admire the symmetry of the quadrangle, nor to dip inside the library to view its treasures, because something much more pressing demanded their attention.

Finally, they had a lead.

A call had come in direct from Mike Nevis, Head of Security at the cathedral, who'd spent some considerable time overnight checking the CCTV footage from the past few days. Much to their collective embarrassment, he had found something before they had.

MacKenzie looked forward to hearing whatever Nevis could tell her, but she also knew that fools rushed in, and so took the trouble to run a quick background check on the man who'd been so eager to make himself a part of their investigation. Michael John Nevis, originally from Berwick-upon-Tweed, was a fifty-one-year-old ex-army corporal, who'd learned about computers during his time serving Her Majesty, and had put his skills to good use since leaving the army with an honourable discharge. He was unmarried, but had two children by different mothers, both of whom had been

149

forced to chase him for child support through the court system. That little nugget prompted a deeper search, which revealed several county court judgments against him for non-payment of finance and other credit agreements in the past three years.

Put together as a whole, it was possible the man had a gambling problem—which was unfortunate, but not particularly interesting, were it not for the bribery risk he now posed. A man in need of a bob or two might find his principles more readily compromised, should the right offer come along. Luckily, before handing over the case, Ryan had had the foresight to request access to bank account data in respect of certain key staff members connected with the cathedral—including Nevis.

"What exactly did he tell you on the phone?" she asked Lowerson, as they approached the north door of the cathedral.

"Nevis said he'd found something suspicious on the footage," Jack replied. "He didn't elaborate, he just said it was urgent."

As they dipped inside the cathedral, the temperature fell by a couple of degrees and MacKenzie shivered. On another day, they might have stopped to admire the perfect lines of arch and column, but they were directed to the security office without delay, where they found Mike Nevis waiting for them.

"Mr Nevis? I'm DI…DCI MacKenzie," she corrected herself. "This is my colleague, DC Lowerson."

"I met a couple of your friends the other day," he said. "Come in."

He closed the door carefully behind them, and they found themselves in a square room dominated by a central, zigzag desk, upon which a number of computer monitors sprouted up like beanstalks.

"It's like a scene from *The Matrix*," Lowerson muttered.

"I understand you'd like to make a report," MacKenzie said, coming straight to the point.

Nevis settled himself on a plush looking desk chair—the kind of high spec model that would never be found inside Northumbria CID—and spread his hands.

"After I sent through the footage to your team, I thought I may as well look over it myself," he said. "To tell you the truth, I was angry to think that I, or one of my team, had missed something. I wanted to check, just to satisfy my own curiosity."

"And? Had you missed something?" MacKenzie asked.

"Obviously, the cameras in the Great Kitchen and the nave were severely compromised by the amount of smoke billowing around those areas, but there are still a few partial images of two people escaping on foot. These two were smart, and they must have known where the cameras were located, because they kept their heads down and their backs to the cameras."

MacKenzie felt her heart plummet. Without a clear image to ID, they would be working with very little.

Or so she believed.

"That isn't really the part I wanted to talk to you about," Nevis said.

He paused to fiddle with the controls.

"The part I want you to see is from a few days prior to the robbery. I've put together a compilation of the clips, to save us some time."

He fiddled with a few buttons, and presently a video began to play on the monitor in front of them.

Moving images rolled across the screen, captured by cameras positioned directly above and to the side of the display case that previously held Cuthbert's cross.

"Here it is," Nevis said quietly. "See?"

MacKenzie gave a slight shake of her head. The images showed a small party of tourists milling around the display case, none of whom appeared particularly out of the ordinary.

"I'm afraid, I don't see—"

Nevis clicked the 'play' button again, and the next set of rolling images, this time captured a few days later, came onto the screen.

"There he is again," Nevis said, and paused the screen.

This time, MacKenzie and Lowerson leaned forward, their eyes scrutinising each face that had frozen on the screen. But it wasn't until Nevis played the third set of images, taken a day after the last, that MacKenzie saw the same thing he had seen.

It was the same man, peering through the display glass at Cuthbert's cross, for several days in a row.

It took another minute for Lowerson to catch up, but, when he did, he gave a low whistle.

"That's the same man," he said.

"I went back over the last two weeks," Nevis said. "Took me all night and most of this morning, but I found him," he said triumphantly. "He isn't a one-off visitor, because he comes back every day, or every other day, for the two weeks leading up to the explosion. I cross-checked some of his visits against footage from the other cameras, but he doesn't linger over any of the other display cases. He comes in and makes directly for the central case holding Cuthbert's cross."

MacKenzie nodded, thinking quickly.

"This is very helpful, Mr Nevis. If you could send this compilation reel straight through to us, that would be even more helpful. We are grateful to you for taking the time to go through the footage; this may well prove to be a vital discovery. We don't know yet, but it is a good lead and we'll follow it up."

She turned to Lowerson.

"Jack, as soon as the compilation footage comes in, I'd like this man's face run through the database to see if we can find any existing match," she said.

It was possible, and the man hadn't been overly cautious to hide his face. She wondered idly whether that was a sign of weakness or confidence.

"Will do," Lowerson said, and moved away to type a quick message to Yates, asking her to expedite the process once the file came through.

"One thing I will say about him," MacKenzie remarked. "Whoever this chap is, he doesn't go to any great lengths to hide his features, does he?"

"Some don't need to," Nevis said. "They move easily with the crowd and blend in. Your colleague was right about that—the first time I looked at this footage, I almost missed him because my eye just passed right over him."

"Which colleague?"

"The tall one—Ryan, was it?"

She smiled.

"Thank you, Mr Nevis."

* * *

Before they went about the rest of their business, MacKenzie turned to Lowerson as soon as they were out of earshot.

"Ask Yates to forward the compilation to Digital Forensics," she said quietly. "I want them to double-check the footage is part of the original and hasn't been doctored."

"D'you think he would do that?"

"A desperate man would do anything," she replied. "Never underestimate the power of fear as a motivating force, Jack."

CHAPTER 21

"Tell us about yourself, Ben."

The three men were seated around a table in one of the smaller meeting rooms at Durham CID, the only concession to informality being the presence of several polystyrene cups.

"There isn't much to know," Carter said. "I'm Benjamin Carter, and I'm twenty-seven years old, but you already know that. My home address is in my personnel file, but I live in the city with my mother, in an apartment building on the river."

"Thank you," Ryan said. "Please, go on."

I joined Durham Constabulary straight after my training at the Police College," Carter said. "Right from the outset, Joan took me under her wing."

He took a minute to compose himself.

"You were close, then?" Phillips asked.

Carter nodded.

"Yes, she had a way of building you up, and being there when you fell," he said. "It's rare to find somebody who's able to do both."

Phillips looked over at his friend, who was entirely unaware that he, too, was one of those rare people. But then, part of being exceptional was not realising you fell into the category.

"How long have you been a sergeant?" Ryan asked.

"Since the end of last year," Carter replied. "I know what you're thinking—and, yes, I am young for the position, but Joan was a woman who rewarded hard work."

Ryan looked for the same quality in his staff, and was struck again by how great a loss Tebbutt would be to the community she had served.

"When was the last time you saw Joan?" Ryan asked.

Carter ran a hand over his mouth, trying to remember.

"It must have been last Friday," he said. "Joan wasn't on duty last Saturday and Sunday, and she regularly opts to take a Monday off work. She used to joke that it was all because of that song by *The Boomtown Rats.*"

"Tell me why I don't like Mondays?" Phillips said.

Carter nodded.

"I know she had a prickly exterior, but, once you got to know her—"

"Once you got to know her dubious taste in music?" Ryan finished for him.

"Dubious?" Phillips almost choked on his coffee. "That song is a classic."

Ryan pinched the bridge of his nose.

"Frank, I am not going to enter into a debate with you about which songs over the entire course of human musical enterprise should count as classics, except to say that the late and great David Bowie would be turning in his grave to hear your say that."

Carter grinned, and then his smile faded.

"We used to have this," he said. "Joan and me, we could have a laugh about life—even on the bad days."

"Like when you had to say goodbye to some of your former colleagues?" Ryan prodded.

"Yeah, those were hard days," he said.

"Which leads us nicely on to my next question," Ryan said. "I know you're already putting together a list of all the people and cases who might have had an axe to grind, and that includes some of your former colleagues. Does anybody in particular stand out to you?"

"There must be a hundred cases," Carter said. "Countless people who threatened her over the years, or had other people do their dirty work for them, but nobody recently springs to mind."

"Nobody at all?"

"When most of the people who used to run Major Crimes were dispatched, that didn't go down well, but she had no choice. People blamed her, but it was the right thing to do."

Carter retrieved printed sheets from his file and slid them across the table.

"I made a list, like you asked. There may be more to add but, quite honestly, searching for the one person amongst this rabble is like searching for the Lost Treasure of Atlantis. When you hunt down the bad guys, you're always running the risk that, one day, one of them will come looking for you."

Not for the first time, Ryan experienced a chill which ran along the length of his spine.

He took the list Carter had prepared.

"A couple of names on here I recognise from Operation Watchman," he said. "Did Joan mention receiving any personal threats?"

Carter shook his head.

"When I saw her last Friday, things were on the up. Violent crime has dipped for the first time in a while," Carter said. "We were celebrating that fact, and looking forward to recruiting some new members of staff. But now—"

"Now, there'll be a job opening," Phillips said, softly.

Carter turned a deep, angry red, which caused his freckles to pop against his pale skin.

"I don't make a habit of jumping into people's graves," he said, and Ryan was intrigued to see another side to the mild-mannered young sergeant.

Interesting.

"Did Joan mention anything to do with the cathedral?" Ryan asked.

Carter appeared to have calmed himself down.

"No, the first she heard about there being anything amiss was when I rang her—"

"You rang her?" Ryan said softly, and leaned forward slightly. "When did you ring her, Ben?

Carter looked between the pair of them like a startled fawn.

I—well, it was just after I heard the news come through from the Control Room about the Durham incident."

"When would that have been?" Phillips asked.

Carter seemed to grow hot, the skin on his forehead turning clammy.

"Around twelve-fifteen," Carter said.

Ryan pinned him with a stare.

"And, tell me, Ben—what time have we established that Joan was killed?"

Carter looked visibly unwell.

"At around twelve-fifteen," he said. "I must have been one of the last people to talk to her. God, I'm sorry, sir—I thought I'd mentioned it already."

Ryan retrieved his file and, with slow and deliberate movements, pulled out the statement Carter had previously provided to Lowerson and Yates.

Time ticked by slowly as Ryan skim-read the document again, then looked up with hard, uncompromising eyes.

"There is no mention of a telephone call in your statement," he said flatly, tapping the document in his hand.

"Would you care to amend it now?" Phillips asked.

Carter nodded.

"Yes, yes of course."

* * *

Later, after Carter left the room on shaking legs, Ryan turned to his sergeant.

"Frank? I don't think we'll wait to see if the key to that drawer is at Tebbutt's house, after all. I want it opened *now*."

Phillips flexed his fingers

"Piece of cake," he said.

CHAPTER 22

At precisely the same moment Phillips was jimmying the lock on Tebbutt's desk drawer, Lowerson took a call from Melanie Yates.

"I've got an ID on that face you sent through," she said.

"That was quick," he replied, and excitement began to stir at the prospect of their first real suspect. "Who is it?"

"Full name, Edward Martin Faber—goes by the street name 'Fabergé'."

"As in, the eggs?"

"I guess so," she said. "Faber used to be a police consultant for the Fraud Team down in Durham, and sometimes in Newcastle. He used to advise on forgery and counterfeiting— that's how we made him so quickly. I've got all the information we need, right here in his file."

"Right now, we only need his address," Lowerson said.

Yates rattled off an address in the village of Burnhope, located halfway between Durham and Consett, and only a short drive away.

"Thanks, Mel, you're a star. I'll keep you posted."

"Try not to have too much fun," she complained. "Some of us are stuck in the office trawling through CCTV footage and statements."

"I'll make it up to you later," he promised.

Then, catching sight of a carved monk who seemed to look down upon him with disapproval, he hastily ended the call. He hurried off in search of MacKenzie, who was in the process of familiarising herself with the cathedral, and found her beside St Cuthbert's shrine. It was resplendent with silk hangings and offerings to the sainted monk.

"They say he's buried underneath here," MacKenzie said, as she heard him approach. "Legend has it, Cuthbert's body remained uncorrupted for an abnormal amount of time after he died, and that helped to fuel all the talk of miracles and healing properties associated with Cuthbert's relics. Everything he owned was considered to have magical healing properties. I can't say I believe in any of that, myself, but at least the robbers only took a golden cross and not the poor man's bones or his coffin."

"I've just had Mel on the phone," he said, no longer able to contain himself. "She's managed to ID our Person of Interest—he's one Edward Faber, street name Fabergé."

The name rang a bell for MacKenzie.

"A few years ago, I was seconded to the Fraud Team for a while," she said. "I think he used to be an informant for them."

"That ties in with what Mel told me," he said. "She says that Faber started out as an informant, and eventually became more of a consultant on counterfeiting investigations."

"It sounds like he may have fallen off the wagon again," MacKenzie said grimly. "I wonder if he had an offer he couldn't refuse."

"Only one way to find out," Lowerson said. "He's living at an address in Burnhope."

"Well, then, let's pay him a friendly visit."

"Yes, ma'am."

* * *

Tebbutt's desk drawer sprang open with a loud metallic twang.

Her colleagues in the Durham Major Crimes Team may have been unhappy at this turn of events, but nobody tried to stop them.

"Right, we're in," Philip said.

Ryan handed over his phone, which he'd been using to record their actions for the case file, and began to rifle through the contents of the drawer.

Tebbutt had been a meticulous woman, even down to the contents of her bottom drawer, which consisted of: a small number of active case files, each clearly marked with a reference number; a small make-up bag containing a selection of personal items, for use in the event that a meeting with the Chief Constable was unexpectedly called; and, a well-worn, leather address book.

That was all.

Ryan bypassed the case files and grasped the book, which contained dozens of entries, each written in a neat curling script with a black pen.

They'd received a message from the Digital Forensics Team to tell them that they'd been able to unlock Tebbutt's mobile phone with the kind help of her daughter, who happened to know the password since it was also her birthday digits. That had enabled the team to access Joan's messages, incoming and outgoing calls, as well as her online searches, which could often be the most illuminating of all.

In this case, she'd received a telephone call the evening before she died, from a number not known to her contacts list. However, the call had lasted almost forty minutes, so there was a strong chance the caller may have been known to her, even if she chose not to keep the number on her list.

Ryan looked down at the address book he held in his hand, and then looked up the mystery number.

It took a few minutes, but eventually he found a match.

"Gotcha," he muttered.

"Got who?" Phillips asked, looking up from his inspection of Joan's active case files.

"You know that mystery caller of Joan's, the night before she died? I've found a match. The entry reads, 'Fabergé', and gives a mobile number and an address in Burnhope."

Phillips rubbed a thoughtful hand over his chin, and cast his mind back.

"Fabergé…that's a name you don't easily forget," he said.

"There were the eggs…"

"I know, but I'm thinking of something else," Phillips said. "I've got a picture in my mind of a weedy-looking bloke with a cleft chin. Used to be an informant, back in the day."

"For Major Crimes?" Ryan asked

"Not in any regular capacity," Phillips said. "I'm positive his line was more to do with fraud."

"We know that Tebbutt started her career on the Fraud Team," Ryan said. "But I don't know why she'd be in contact with this man still, unless she had a case where the need arose for her to reach out to him."

"Maybe we should pay this Fabergé a visit and ask him to explain it to us?" Phillips said. "Burnhope isn't far from here, and it's on the way back to Durham."

Ryan slotted the drawer back into place and stretched a line of police tape across the top, to seal the entrance.

"Come on, Frank. The game's afoot."

* * *

Ryan and Phillips raced along the country lanes from Durham Constabulary Headquarters towards the village of Burnhope with what some might have said was a blatant disregard for the highway code.

"Here, man, go canny!" Phillips cried, bracing his knee against the dashboard.

"Anna tells me to speed up, you tell me to slow down—there's no pleasing some people," Ryan said, as they barrelled around another sharp corner.

"You've perked up, haven't you?" Phillips said. "Yesterday, you were as flat as a fart, but now you're as happy as Larry."

Ryan grinned at his sergeant's inimitable turn of phrase.

"Must be the pleasure of your company," he said, and realised it was true. Frank Phillips was always a tonic, in every scenario. "Thanks for your support, these past couple of days."

Phillips waved that away.

"Don't mention it," he said. "Besides, I like the stotties in the hospital canteen."

"Ah, well, that explains it."

Soon, they turned off the main road and passed by a large iron pit-wheel sculpture marking the entrance to the village, which was a nod to the area's rich mining history. Like much of the county and, indeed, the country, Burnhope was a place of contrast. Large new-builds overlooked old rows of pit cottages which had once housed coal miners and their families, and where community pride was still a living, breathing thing.

Faber had one of the new-build properties, which spoke of his moderate success in the field of counterfeiting, before a midlife crisis of integrity had coincided with an unfortunate bust-up with the local police, forcing him to re-examine his life choices.

The house was a linear, two-storey affair, with a small front garden and a slightly larger one to the rear There was a single car on the driveway—a classic 1970s Mini, which Anna would have loved, being a fan of the little cars herself.

Ryan followed a neat flagstone pathway and knocked loudly at the front door.

When there was no answer, he cocked his ear to the wood and listened for any sound of movement within.

Phillips peered through the downstairs bay window, but could see no signs of life.

Ryan tried again, knocking more loudly this time.

"Are you looking for Eddie?"

They turned to find one of his neighbours hovering at the bottom of the paved driveway, dressed in her nurse's uniform, which told them she'd either just finished or was about to begin her shift.

"Yes," Ryan said. "Any idea where he might be?"

"Haven't seen him for a few days," the neighbour said, *shushing* the dog which tugged impatiently at its lead.

Ryan and Phillips exchanged a worried glance. After all, the man's car was still sitting on the driveway.

It didn't add up.

"If you happen to see him, tell him Angie's asking after him," the woman said.

As she wandered off, Ryan thought that, no matter how shady a life Edward Faber had led, he had still been able to find friendship.

It was a heartening thought.

"What do you reckon?" Phillips said.

Ryan squinted through the porthole window in the front door, and heaved a gusty sigh.

"I reckon we better put some shoe coverings on, Frank."

"I was worried you might say that," Phillips grumbled.

* * *

They tried the front door a couple more times, before deciding to make their way to the back of the house, where they found the white UPVC back door hanging limply from its hinges.

Both men went on high alert.

"On my signal," Ryan said, positioning himself beside the broken door.

"Mr Faber!" he called out. "This is the police! We have reason to believe your life is in danger! Please be advised we intend to enter the property!"

He waited a beat, but when there were still no signs of life, Ryan held up three fingers of his left hand to signal a countdown.

"Three...two...one!"

Ryan planted his boot against the kitchen door and thrust into the house, with Phillips hard at his heels.

"Police! Police!" Ryan called out the standard alert, but he knew almost immediately that there would be no reply.

The air was saturated with something ripe and rancid, mingled with the tinny scent of blood. It clung to their nostrils and caused them to retch as the two men searched the downstairs rooms, watchful for any signs of life. There was a curious stillness to the house that Ryan would always associate with death; a kind of netherworld, where a soul had departed, but the body remained.

The smell grew stronger as they reached the hallway, and Phillips cast his eyes towards the ceiling.

"Upstairs," he said, and pulled an expressive face.

"After you," Ryan agreed, gesturing for Phillips to precede him.

"No, no, after *you*," Phillips said.

Shaking his head, Ryan led the way up a narrow flight of carpeted stairs, with Phillips following at a more stately pace behind.

The air grew even more stagnant as they emerged onto the landing, and Ryan raised his hand to signal caution. Blood spatter had reached the carpet directly outside the bathroom, where the light had been left to burn.

No prizes for guessing where they'd find Faber.

Still, they checked the bedrooms first, and only when they were sure nobody else was inside the house did they eventually turn their minds to the one room they hadn't explored.

When they did, they wished they hadn't.

Both men said nothing while their bodies adjusted to the horror, struggling to control the strong urge to reject what their eyes could see, all too clearly.

"Good God," Phillips whispered, holding his sleeve against his mouth to mask the fetid odour of human waste.

Ryan said nothing at all, his face shuttered. Calm grey eyes swept over the bathroom, noting the tiny details that would later torment him.

"Whoever did this washed themselves in the shower, afterwards," he said, nodding towards a separate, freestanding cubicle which was the only thing in the room without any blood spatter. "The carpet out here is relatively clean, so they must have brought spare clothing, or covered their shoes."

Phillips was breathing hard through his teeth.

"Is it definitely Faber?" he asked.

It was by no means obvious.

"Yes, I think so," Ryan replied, and forced himself to look again at the remains inside the bathtub.

Whoever killed Edward Faber had really gone to town.

CHAPTER 23

MacKenzie and Lowerson parked at the opposite end of the street and made their way towards Edward Faber's front door, drawing a very curious expression from a passing dog walker, who paused at the end of the driveway.

"My, Eddie's getting popular," she called out. "You're the second lot I've seen today."

"Isn't Eddie home?" MacKenzie called back.

"No, I was just telling those other two men, I haven't seen Eddie in a few days."

MacKenzie and Lowerson felt a trickle of alarm.

"What did these other two men look like?" MacKenzie asked.

"Oh, quite hard and serious," the neighbour said. "My eyesight isn't what it used to be, but I'd say one of them was tall and athletic, and the other a bit shorter and, you know, stocky. Built like a fighter. Why? Is Eddie in some kind of bother? This is the third visit he's had in the space of a week, and that's more than he usually has in a whole year."

"Did you see Eddie leaving with these two men?" Lowerson asked, imagining Faber being hauled off by a couple of hired thugs.

"No, I was off walking Mutley, and I've only just come back. I don't know what happened to them, but they were polite enough."

"Thanks for your help," MacKenzie said.

Once the neighbour had moved off again, she turned to Jack.

"I have a mind to call in some backup," she said. "Something smells off, especially since there have been others sniffing around."

"Can't see anything through the window," Lowerson said, pressing his nose to the glass as Phillips had done so recently. "Why don't we try around the back?"

MacKenzie thought about it, then nodded.

"Probably best not to alert anyone by ringing the bell," she said. "If Faber is home, he can come to the back door and, if he's in trouble, we can enter without causing too much alarm."

Lowerson caught a quick flash of pain crossing her face as her foot caught on the edge of a flagstone, and reached out to help her.

"Careful," he said. "Here, take my hand—"

"No," she said, sharply. "No, I'm fine, Jack. I'll be fine."

* * *

Edward Faber had not died well. His body had been dumped unceremoniously into his bathtub, which Phillips happened to notice was one of those fancy affairs with the jet stream bubbles. This had been neither quick nor easy, judging by the fingers missing from his right hand, which was—like the rest of his body—in the throes of decomposition.

"Looks like the poor bastard's been tortured," Phillips said.

"They water-boarded him first," Ryan said. "They left the bucket and towel over there."

Phillips followed his gaze to where a bright-red bucket stood incongruously in the corner of the room, with a sodden towel hanging out of it. Elsewhere, blood was spattered over much of the tiles and walls, which probably reflected the heavy injuries sustained to the man's head and torso.

"How long do you think he's been gone?" Phillips asked.

"Judging by the stage of putrefaction, I'd say at least three or four days," Ryan replied. "If he put a call through to Tebbutt on Sunday night, it can't have been before then, but Pinter will be able to give us a better idea."

He thought of what kind of mind was capable of inflicting injuries such as these, and then answered his own question. He knew exactly the kind of mind; he'd encountered them, many times before. Morally absent, entirely without remorse, and often children of extreme abuse who'd grown into adults without empathy. For a certain brand of criminal, it could be a very lucrative trait to possess.

"At least this answers one question," he said.

Phillips, who'd been forced to step away or lose his lunch, raised an eyebrow.

"What's that?"

"The question of whether there's a connection between Tebbutt's murder and the robbery at the cathedral. Now we know there *has* to be. It's no mere coincidence that this man called Tebbutt, and they both ended up dead."

Just then, they heard a sound downstairs.

Ryan tapped his fingers to his lips. If the same people who'd done this to Edward Faber had returned to the scene, they wouldn't be the friendly types, judging by their recent handiwork.

"Quick—the spare bedroom," he whispered, and both men concealed themselves behind its closed door.

* * *

"Did you hear something?"

MacKenzie and Lowerson stood completely still in the kitchen downstairs, listening for any sounds of life.

"Probably just a creak," he said.

They continued to search the downstairs rooms, wrinkling their noses at the cloying stench of death.

"D'you think—?"

"Yes," MacKenzie said shortly. "Somebody has died in this house. We follow procedure, and make sure nobody else is alive or injured, before tending to any body or bodies we may find."

Eventually, she put her foot on the bottom stair and squared her shoulders, dragging herself upward and into the unknown. Lowerson followed, dreading whatever awaited them in the shadows upstairs, and grateful he did not have to face it alone.

"In here," she said, as she caught sight of the open bathroom door at the top of the landing.

She looked inside, and then quickly away again.

"Best prepare yourself, Jack. It's not a pretty sight."

But before he could look, there came another creak from one of the bedrooms.

MacKenzie was angry with herself for not checking those rooms first, and prayed whoever was in there wasn't carrying.

"Go and call for back-up," she ordered.

"Not a chance," Lowerson said, surprising her. "I'm not leaving you here, alone."

"Alright, we go together. We're unarmed, so we retreat."

They didn't make it far before the bedroom door swung open and a dark figure loomed, poised for attack.

* * *

"AAARGH!"

Lowerson let out an undignified yell, which soon evaporated on the air as he caught sight of the two men emerging from one of Faber's spare bedrooms.

"*Frank*? For the love of all that's holy—you nearly gave me a heart attack! What the hell are you two doing here?" MacKenzie cried.

"We could ask the same of you," Ryan replied. "Why were you both creeping around, anyway?"

MacKenzie stuck a hand on her hip and used the other to point an accusing finger in his direction.

"Never mind what *we* are doing here," she said. "We were following a lead in the cathedral case. Now, I have no idea how you found out about Faber, but I thought it was understood that we would keep the two investigations separate, and your involvement in the case to an absolute minimum?"

Ryan held up his hands in a gesture of surrender.

"I swear, we're here because we were following a lead in the Tebbutt case," he said. "Faber put a call through to Joan Tebbutt the night before she died. We wanted to come and ask him why, that's all."

MacKenzie felt her heart rate return to normal.

"We've just come from the cathedral," she said. "Their Head of Security is a proactive type, and took it upon himself to start analysing the CCTV footage."

"Mike Nevis? Yeah, he has that look about him. Just so long as he doesn't tamper with it, we can use all the help we can get," Ryan remarked.

"My thoughts exactly," MacKenzie said. "Anyway, Faber turned up on the footage several times, he visited the cathedral on consecutive days in the lead up to the robbery on Monday, and always to see St Cuthbert's cross."

"Sounds fishy," Phillips said, vocalising what they were all thinking.

"The thought had crossed my mind," MacKenzie said.

Phillips nodded his head towards the bathroom door.

"We'll have a hard job asking him anything, now," he said. "The bloke's well and truly kicked the bucket."

Ryan laughed, despite the circumstances.

"Nicely put, as always, Frank."

"One tries, dear boy."

* * *

While Phillips and Lowerson dealt with the practicalities of calling in the murder and enlisting the assistance of the coroner's office and Faulkner's team of CSIs, Ryan and MacKenzie compared notes.

"You said from the beginning that the two cases would be linked," MacKenzie said. "The problem now is trying to figure out *how* they connect."

Ryan watched a sparrow swoop down to peck at something only it could see, before rising up again with an elegant flap of wings.

"Faber—or Fabergé—must have been in league with the robbers," Ryan said. "He has form, and the necessary connections, although I wouldn't have said he was in the Big Leagues."

MacKenzie mulled it over. "Set against that was Faber's longstanding relationship with the police in this neck of the woods," she said. "He was a trusted informant and even a consultant on some cases. He must have known he'd be in the frame if he got on board with something like that."

"Then, there's the phone call to Tebbutt on Sunday night," Ryan said. "Why call Tebbutt, unless it was to turn himself in?"

They heard the arrival of police responders, followed by the sound of Phillips voice reverberating around the quiet cul-de-sac as he directed them to start securing the scene.

"There's another thing to consider," Ryan said, thinking of the kind of woman Tebbutt had been. "If Faber had called to tell Joan of the plan for Monday's robbery, she would have done everything in her power to prevent it from happening. So why didn't she? Obviously, because she didn't expect it to happen on that particular day or because Faber didn't know the precise day it was due to happen. After all, he can't have been part of the crew who committed the actual theft—he was already dead by then, as we now know."

MacKenzie thought of the man lying upstairs, and then of his house.

"The house has been ransacked," she said. "Very tidily done, I must say, but there were drawers not fully pushed in and a couple of doors half open in the kitchen. I wouldn't be surprised to find similar things upstairs."

Come to think of it, Ryan thought, she was right.

"They were obviously looking for something, and perhaps they tortured Faber to try to elicit its whereabouts. It couldn't have been the cross, because it wasn't stolen until Monday. Unless the torture was a punishment for speaking to Joan Tebbutt."

MacKenzie shook her head.

"This is all conjecture," she said. "What could they have been looking for?"

"That's the question."

CHAPTER 24

Anna dreamed of the island.

She felt the sand crush between her toes as she walked along the harbour beach, and felt the sting of the wind against her cheeks as she stopped to look across the sea to Bamburgh castle. She smiled as the late afternoon sun burnished its stone a deep orange-red, a beacon against the crashing waves of the sea far below.

She walked on, waving to the children she'd once known, seeing herself and Megan amongst them.

Megan.

She watched her sister's dark hair whip around her face as a woman's voice called to them on the wind.

Anna! Megan! Time to come home!

She saw two little girls sprint across the sand into their mother's waiting arms and smiled, just for a moment, before the scene changed as she knew it would.

The wind began to pick up, curling the waves into breaking arches against the sand as she remained there, afraid to walk on, afraid to see.

The wind was howling now, rushing through the village streets.

Louder and louder it wailed, until it no longer sounded like the rush of a breeze but the cry of a woman's voice in terror.

Anna tried to run, but found she couldn't move.

Andy, no!

She tried to raise her hands, to cover her ears, but they too were frozen, trapped in the capsule of a memory she could no longer control.

Then, she saw a man walking towards her, dressed in long, simple robes. Around his neck hung a glittering cross, no longer roughened or worn, but new. In one hand, he carried a string of fish, and, in the other, something she could not make out.

Help! Help me, please!

As the wind roared on, her head began to throb, the pain too intense to bear. Tears began to fall, mingling with the rain which plastered her hair and ran in rivulets down her pale face.

The man drew nearer, and the wind stopped suddenly.

Overhead, clouds continued to swirl darkly, and on the far horizon, old-fashioned cargo ships tipped and bobbed to the mood of the sea. But there on the sand, the rain stopped and all became silent, as though the world was waiting for him to speak.

Are you penitent, my child?

The clouds parted to allow a shaft of light, which illuminated the man's face.

But it was not Cuthbert, nor any other kindly saint come to help her.

It was him.

The face she would always see, in the depths of her nightmares.

Her father's face.

Stephen Walker's face.

Mark Fowler's face.

Keir Edward's face.

I am The Master, he said. *Welcome to my Circle.*

In his arms, he held a baby girl.

* * *

Eve and Charles heard Anna screaming, and ran as fast as they could.

"Shh, there, you're safe, Anna. You're safe," Ryan's mother crooned, running a gentle hand over her daughter-in-law's face.

"Charles, fetch some water and a facecloth, please," she said. "Anna? It's me. It's Eve."

Anna swam back to the surface like a drowning woman, gasping for breath as she sought to escape the world her mind had conjured, trying to claw her way out, kicking at the covers with her one good leg.

"You were having a nightmare," Eve said, rubbing her hand. "It's over, now. You're home, in Elsdon, and safe with us here."

She dabbed the tears away from Anna's eyes with a tissue and, a moment later, Charles returned with water, a facecloth, and a dram of whisky.

Eve raised an eyebrow at that.

"It's medicinal," he said, defensively.

"Thank you," Anna said. "I—I'm sorry, I can't seem to sit up."

"Let me help you."

Eve and Charles helped to lift her up, propping some pillows behind her head and checking the bandages hadn't been dislodged in the process. They elevated her broken ankle on another pillow on the bed, and righted the bedclothes, which had fallen to the floor.

"How's the pain?" Charles asked.

Anna gave him a weak smile.

"I've felt better," she admitted. "Sorry to cause such a fuss."

"You didn't cause a fuss," Eve said. "We were worried about you."

"You were shouting about something to do with a circle," Charles said. "Is that the same Circle you had trouble with, a few years ago?"

Anna took a sip of the water Eve offered, along with the painkillers to ease the pain in her head.

"It's an old nightmare," she said. "Usually, I relive the experience I had with the cult, and I see my father, or one of the other leaders, dressed in their animal masks and long black robes. This time, it was slightly different. I saw a man who I thought was Saint Cuthbert, but he turned into something else, something monstrous, and called himself 'Master'."

"What happened to you in Durham is bound to stir things up again," Eve said. "I'll call Ryan—"

"No, please, I don't want him to worry," Anna said. "It was a bad nightmare, that's all. I'll tell him about it when he comes home, but there's nothing he can do now. Besides, what I really want is for him to find the people who did this and get them off the streets, before anybody else is hurt. It'll make him feel better, knowing the world is balanced again."

Charles smiled.

"You know him very well, don't you? Max…that is, Ryan was always that way. Always eager to see justice done, and always so upset when he uncovered a fresh injustice in the world."

"It's because he's an idealist," Anna said, closing her eyes against the glare of the sun through the bedroom window. "He wants to make the world the best it can be."

Charles nodded, remembering a time when he'd been the same.

"I'll make some sandwiches," he said, to change the subject. "You need fattening up."

With that, he was gone, leaving the two women staring at an open doorway.

"They're so similar, aren't they?" Anna said. "Ryan has a habit of command that would be incredibly aggravating, if he didn't have so many redeeming features."

"Ryan and Charles? Yes, they're much more similar than they know," Eve said quietly. "I'm afraid he gets that habit of command from his father. Mind you, I've found that all it takes is a firm stick and a juicy carrot to keep things ticking along nicely."

They both laughed at the metaphor.

"I won't ask what kind of carrot," Anna said.

"That's for the best, dear."

CHAPTER 25

It was a small party who gathered together in one of the conference rooms at Northumbria CID for a five o'clock briefing, Phillips having already taken himself off to collect Samantha from school, thereby giving his wife the time to manage her side of the investigation. Likewise, Chief Constable Morrison had elected not to attend owing to a number of other pressing engagements, leaving only Ryan, MacKenzie, Lowerson and one or two support staff in attendance.

It was almost ten minutes past the hour, and Yates remained notably absent.

"Anybody know what's happened to Mel?" Ryan asked.

Lowerson, who would be the most likely to know her whereabouts, was at a loss.

"I'll try calling her again," he said. "It isn't like her to be late."

"In the meantime, we'll make a start," Ryan said, and invited MacKenzie to take the floor.

"Thanks," she said, turning to the group. "I know it's getting late in the day, so I'll make this brief. What we've learned is that whoever orchestrated the robbery at the cathedral on Monday was meticulous. They did their homework—for example, they knew they wouldn't be able to carry any of their improvised smoke devices through the baggage check into the Open Galleries. They knew this would present a problem, since they would need the

182

smoke to act as both cover and diversion while they tore into the display case to steal the cross, so they came up with solutions."

She moved around the desk to where a large-scale schematic diagram of Durham Cathedral had been pinned to the whiteboard.

"Thanks to the efforts of DC Yates—alongside our analytical support staff, who've been working tirelessly to piece together the CCTV footage received from the cathedral and other external sources—we've been able to build up a clearer picture of how the robbers went about their business on Monday."

She moved along the board to where two partial images of the robbers had been displayed.

"In the first place, we know there were at least two robbers working in tandem. One, who planted the devices"—she rapped a knuckle against the first image—"and another, who brazenly wandered into the open galleries through the baggage check, just like any regular tourist."

She moved to the second image, which consisted of a side-view of somebody's head, too generic to provide any determinative identification, despite all the technology at their disposal.

"The first man—or, person we *believe* to be a man, factoring in average height and build—set about planting the first three smoke devices in the main part of the cathedral. He left two beneath the pews in the nave, and another underneath the font, right in front of the entrance at the north door."

Arrogant, Ryan thought. For any would-be criminal to act in such a risky fashion displayed an extraordinarily high level of arrogance—or, he supposed, a very high level of motivation. It was a dangerous combination, whichever way you looked at it.

"These three devices were detonated first, by some remote method, probably a mobile phone," MacKenzie was saying. "Then, as visitors and staff reacted to the shock of the first three explosions, this first robber made his way quickly to the exit of the Open Galleries, which leads directly into the Great Kitchen. Once he was sure his accomplice was already in place beside the display cabinet housing Cuthbert's cross, he proceeded to throw another smoke bomb inside the gallery area, setting off the alarm and creating further panic. It was this second, slightly delayed detonation that Dr Taylor Ryan heard and, as smoke gradually began to fill the room, she found herself in the path of the second robber, whose sole purpose it was to break into the display case using an axe which had been thrown inside for him to use. In all, we calculate there was less than a thirty-second time lag between the first and second detonations."

"Slick and well organised," Ryan put in. "Don't underestimate the people we're dealing with. These are hardened criminals, not bumbling amateurs—and they have no remorse."

MacKenzie thought of her friend stumbling through the fog, only to be struck a brutal blow to the back of her head with the butt of the robbers' axe. She hoped it was footage Ryan never watched, because it made for traumatic viewing.

She drew in a long breath, and began again.

"The first robber, having now completed his task, re-joined the rest of the crowd and made his way back outside into the afternoon sunshine, while his friend did the same less than a minute later. To understand where they went next, DC Yates sought the assistance of Durham City Council, who've provided us with extensive access to their CCTV and ANPR network."

She referred to the traffic monitoring system used by the city council to monitor all vehicles entering and leaving the city via the main roads.

"Mike Nevis, who is the Head of Security at the cathedral has been especially helpful, and has provided us with extensive footage from their own security network. Thanks to the efforts of all these people, we were able to trace the robbers' movements as far as Prebends Bridge, and then we believe either or both of them made off in a stolen Citroen Picasso, which was reported missing on Monday morning before the robbery took place, and was recovered later in the day from a dump site near the motorway."

She waited to see if there were any questions, before continuing.

"That's where the trail runs cold—"

Just then, Yates burst into the room, breathing heavily.

"I'm sorry I'm late," she said, in a rush of words. "I've been following a new lead."

Heads turned in Mel's direction, her tardiness immediately forgiven.

"What lead?" MacKenzie asked. "I don't know if Jack managed to tell you, but Edward Faber was found dead—"

"I heard," Yates said, with less sympathy than she might usually feel, considering the urgency of the moment. "It isn't about Faber, ma'am."

She swallowed nerves.

"I know where the robbers are, ma'am."

* * *

Ryan was the first to react.

"How?" he said, urgently. "How can you be sure, Mel?"

If he was to put together a task force, with firearms support, then he needed to be certain.

Several pairs of eyes turned to where Yates hovered in the doorway, and she battled a rising tide of nerves that threatened to take a stranglehold.

"Well, sir, when I was looking into tracing the robbers' vehicle earlier today, I had an idea…"

"Go on," he urged.

"The Citroen Picasso was stolen from a quiet residential street to the west of the city," she said. "Whichever robber was responsible for stealing the car, it's likely he or she would have had a mobile phone in their possession. Mobile phones use the nearest mast to transmit from, and they do this automatically, scanning the vicinity for the nearest signal as we move about. So, it occurred to me that, if we could only get a list of all the mobile phone numbers that were transmitting from the mast nearest the location where the car was stolen, we could compare it with the list of phone numbers that were *also* transmitting later that day, from the mast nearest the location where the car was dumped."

"Surely there would be thousands of mobile phones transmitting to a data mast at any one time," MacKenzie said.

Yates nodded.

"That's right, and there were over 200,000 numbers transmitting to the data mast nearest the address where the Citroen Picasso was stolen. There were even more numbers transmitting to the data mast nearest the site where the car was dumped. However, after receiving the data, the Digital Forensics Team were able to input the data into a specialist program to compare the two lists to find a match. There was only one mobile phone number which appeared on both lists for the relevant timeframes, and we found it."

Lowerson's face broke into a broad grin.

"You're a genius, Mel!" he said. "It sounds so simple when you say it like that, because you're right. The robber is the only one whose phone would be transmitting from both locations on the same day, around the times we think the car was stolen and later dumped."

Yates nodded.

"Exactly. I worked on the basis that the Citroen was stolen sometime between six and eight in the morning on Monday, according to its owner. That gave us a useful window to work with. Likewise, to drive from Durham to the dump site would have taken no more than fifteen minutes. That being the case, we can estimate the Citroen was abandoned at around twelve-thirty, or thereabouts."

"You said you know where these people are," MacKenzie reminded her. "How did you manage to get an address?"

"Once I had the unique mobile phone number, I was able to contact the phone service provider, who told me which mast is currently being used for transmission. Actually, they used the nearest three masts to triangulate the position as accurately as possible. That's how I know they're at a farmhouse just south of Hamsterley Forest, off Windy Bank Road—or, at least, their mobile phone is there."

Ryan couldn't have felt prouder of her, and of his team, than in that single defining moment.

"This kind of dedication and resourcefulness deserves a commendation," he told her. "I'll speak to the Chief Constable first thing tomorrow."

"And I'll second it," McKenzie said.

"Until then, what are we waiting for?" Ryan asked the room at large. "Let's *move!*"

CHAPTER 26

W indy Side Farm was located on the southern edge of Hamsterley Forest, the largest woodland area in the county and home to more than two thousand hectares of trees and wildlife. It lay to the west of the A1 motorway, which sliced through the county and divided it into two parts; the heritage coast to the east, and the forests and open moorland to the west.

Windy Bank Road ran parallel to the southernmost edge of the forest, in an elevated position from which its name was derived. The neighbouring forest attracted hordes of visitors during busy times but, at other times, it could be a lonely, barren place, providing seclusion to anybody seeking to lose themselves within the protective fold of the valley.

Having sought and been given immediate approval to execute a raid on the farmhouse, Ryan and MacKenzie had mustered a small taskforce, consisting of their immediate team, with the support of specialist firearms officers who would take up strategic positions around the perimeter. It was true that Ryan, Phillips and MacKenzie had each received firearms training, but they were firmly of the opinion that discharging a weapon was a matter best left to the specialists and, even then, only as a last resort.

In the present circumstances, considering the scale and aggravated nature of the robbery at the cathedral, the associated risk that firearms might be used against them was considerably higher than usual. Though every member of Ryan's team was kitted out in protective gear, it would be foolish to pretend that there was not a greater element of risk involved in the raid, especially in conditions of low visibility. More so than ever before, Ryan was reminded of how the decisions he took now might affect the future.

His marriage to Anna was based on the tenets of truth and honesty at all times, including his being open about moments when he was required to put himself in danger in the line of duty.

Before going any further, he called his wife.

"Ryan residence," his father answered.

Did people still answer the phone like that?

Apparently so.

"It's me," he said. "Is Anna there? I'd like to speak to her, if she's awake, and up to it."

Charles went off to check, but soon returned to say that she'd been exhausted that day, and was already fast asleep.

"In that case, don't wake her," Ryan said. "If she asks for me later, tell her I'll be home as soon as I can."

As a career diplomat, Charles Ryan was supremely adept at reading between the lines of what people said and didn't say. It was easier to judge non-verbal signals when talking face-to-face, but it was equally possible to hear the change in vocal tone and speech pattern when using the phone.

In this case, he heard a measure of fear in his son's voice, no matter how Ryan tried to hide it.

"Good luck," he said. "Don't worry about Anna, she's safe here with us. Focus on yourself, and on getting the job done."

Ryan didn't stop to wonder how his father knew of his internal conflict; some things were just instinct, he supposed.

"I will," he said. "Thanks."

* * *

The scenery passed by in a blur as Ryan, Lowerson and Yates made the bumpy journey from CID Headquarters to their rendezvous point near Windy Side Farm. It was agreed that MacKenzie would remain back at base, directing operations via radio and acting as a point of contact with the Chief Constable. Though she understood the sense of it, there was a time not so long ago when she would have been the first to volunteer for a field operation, and she felt the loss of liberty very keenly.

The farm was accessible over the fields on foot, or via two roads on either side of the property running along the eastern and western edges of the farmland. Firearms support officers were stationed on either side, and it was agreed that Lowerson and Yates would station themselves with Team A to the west, while Ryan would station himself with Team B, to the east.

"ETA three minutes," MacKenzie said, her soft Irish burr sounding out over the radio. "Take your positions."

They reached the edge of the farm shortly before seven o'clock, as the sun went down on the people of County Durham and made way for a harvest moon. It lit up the valley, spotlighting the old, ramshackle farmhouse and its small collection of outhouses. A single car was parked on the grassy track—they could not call it a driveway—leading up to the main farmhouse, which was in darkness aside from a single light which burned in one of the downstairs rooms.

Once they were in position, Ryan took out his night-vision glasses and tried to get a better view, seeking out the heat sources to better plan their approach.

But there were no heat sources.

Ryan frowned, then tried again, with no better result.

He reached for his radio.

"No clear view of any heat source from the east," he said. "What about from the west?"

Lowerson had been experiencing the same momentary confusion, having expected to find at least two detectable heat sources inside the farmhouse.

"No heat sources from this vantage point, either," he said.

Back at Headquarters, MacKenzie advised caution.

"Just because you can't see them, doesn't mean they aren't there," she said. "Approach with care."

Ryan agreed.

"Advance with extreme caution," he said. "On my mark."

They moved like dark spectres across the fields, keeping to the hedgerows and out of the path of the wind, which circled the valley basin and rushed upward to howl through the forest, sending the trees swaying back and forth against the inky-blue skyline.

Soon enough, they neared the house and Ryan took out his field goggles again.

There was still no discernible heat source, apart from the approaching cluster of bodies from the west, who were already accounted for.

A slow feeling of dread began to creep its way through Ryan's system, warning him clearly of what was to come.

Death.

But not his own.

* * *

They approached the farmhouse from all sides, fanning out as they drew near, keeping themselves low to the ground. The darkness was all-encompassing and, had it not been for the moonlight, they might have tripped over the body lying face down in the grass directly outside the front door, which stood open to the night and creaked loudly on its rusted hinges.

The man who had, albeit briefly, held Cuthbert's cross in his avaricious hands—the same hands that had dealt Anna a blow that had almost robbed her of life—had died following a single penetrating gunshot wound to the head, fired at close range. Though they didn't yet fully understand how Tebbutt's murder related to the cathedral robbery, if this man who now lay before them had taken any part in her demise, then there was certainly a dark irony to the manner of his own death. He had, most likely, died instantaneously, but where they could find pity in their hearts and take comfort from such knowledge in the case of their friend and colleague, it was considerably harder to apply the same logic to a man who had been responsible for such suffering and for whom they'd envisaged a very different outcome.

Firearms officers swept the farmhouse and, after pronouncing it safe to enter, Ryan, Lowerson and Yates stepped over the threshold.

Inside, it was clear that the place had already been searched and, unlike Faber's home, there had been no effort made to disguise the fact. The furnishings were expensive but dated, suggesting that it must have been some time since the house was in regular use. But now, the cushions were torn, their fillings laid bare and hanging like cotton entrails across the floor. Drawers had been displaced, their meagre contents lying scattered over a threadbare rug. In the kitchen, once the heart of the home, what few utensils there were now lay on the dusty floor beside the rubbish, which had been tipped out of the bin and scattered over the floor.

They walked through the empty house, remaining cautious as they moved from room to room, stepping over shards of broken glass and torn cloth.

"They were looking for something, but couldn't find it," Ryan said. "It must have been the cross."

"They've turned the whole place upside down," Lowerson agreed. "Perhaps the guy outside tried to hide the loot and keep it all for himself, so the other one turned on him."

"They do say there's no honour among thieves," Yates said.

Ryan continued to prowl around the courtyard outside, peering inside the car before opening one of the doors and shining his torch light around the interior.

"I need more light over here," he said, and the other two hurried over.

"They searched in here, too," Ryan said, taking in the torn seats and ripped carpet in the footwells.

"They searched everywhere," Lowerson said. "They must have found whatever they were looking for. There's nowhere left to look."

Ryan walked around the outside of the car, lifting the boot to peer inside, then dropping down to peer beneath the undercarriage.

He was about to agree with Jack's statement and suggest they call in reinforcements to deal with the body, when his eye fell on one part of the car which did not appear to have been tampered with.

Fuel cap.

Ryan pressed a hand to the cover and it popped open, sending something wrapped in cloth tumbling to the floor at his feet with a light *thud*.

"Light!" Ryan said. "Shine a light over here!"

There, glowing in the darkness, was Cuthbert's cross.

CHAPTER 27

It was after eleven by the time Ryan made it home to Elsdon. He'd overseen the transfer of the cross into the hands of an expert at Durham University, who would authenticate it and return it to the cathedral as soon as possible. Meanwhile, Lowerson and Yates had supervised the crime scene and the CSIs, whose good humour at being called out so late in the day was testament to their civic pride and willingness to do their part in bringing an end to what had been an extraordinary turn of events.

When Ryan tiptoed upstairs, he expected to find his wife fast asleep. Sleep was the best medicine to speed her recovery but, apparently, it was easier said than done, judging by the small avalanche of books spread out on the bed beside her.

The one she happened to be reading was propped up against her bump, so she could read more easily, and her profile was silhouetted by the warm glow of the bedside lamp. She could often be found reading in bed with a cup of tea by her side and he was glad that, despite all the bandages and bruises, she was still his Anna.

When she spotted him in the doorway, her face broke into a smile.

"Ryan," she said.

He crossed the room in a few strides and sank onto the bed beside her. He brushed his lips over hers with infinite care, and then leaned down to press another kiss to her stomach.

"I thought you'd be asleep by now," he said.

"I couldn't," she said. "I had a nightmare, earlier today, and my subconscious hasn't quite recovered from it yet."

"What nightmare?" he asked, full of concern. As somebody who suffered from night terrors himself, he didn't try to downplay their effect.

"A variation on the usual," she said. "Except, this time, there was a man dressed in a monk's robes, not black ceremonial ones, like the Circle used to wear."

She referred to the cult which had spread its poison far and wide, corrupting men and women from the highest to the lowest echelons, her own father included.

"Perhaps the robed figure represented Cuthbert?"

"That's what I thought at first," Anna said. "But then the face changed and became something hideous. Then, it told me it was the Master and, Ryan, it…that *thing* was holding our baby—"

Her voice quivered on the last word, and he touched his forehead very gently to hers, holding her close.

"It sounds awful," he said. "I wish you'd called me."

"I didn't want you to be interrupted today," she said. "I heard about the other body, in Burnhope, and I knew you'd have a lot to do."

"I didn't think it would take a long for the media to catch up."

"Nobody seems to know why he died," Anna said.

Ryan had a few theories of his own, but he was not about to share them just before bed. Besides, he was glad to be the bearer of good tidings, for once.

Anna gave a huge, jaw-cracking yawn.

"How did your raid go?" she asked.

"We were hoping to take the robbers unawares, and then bring them in to squeeze them a bit, under caution," he said. "Unfortunately, when we arrived at the farm where they'd been hiding out, one was dead and the other missing."

"Oh," she said, full of sympathy. "I'm sorry it was a wasted trip. Do you think one killed the other?"

"Mmm," he said, and rose from the bed to strip off his clothes. "We think one planned to double-cross the other, and, when the other found out about that, he cut his friend out of the deal permanently and then tried to find where he'd hidden the cross."

"The other robber must be miles away by now," she said. "Off to hand over the cross to his client, or whoever put them up to this in the first place, in exchange for a big wad of cash."

"I doubt that," he said. "I doubt that very much, considering I found the cross hidden inside the fuel cap of the dead man's car. It's already in the hands of one of your colleagues from the university, who'll authenticate it as quickly as possible and return it to its rightful place at the cathedral."

In her excitement, Anna tried to sit up too quickly.

"That's *wonderful*," she exclaimed. "You don't know what this will mean to people—"

"I know what it means to you," he said softly.

"It isn't about a bit of old gold," she said. "It is about people's heritage, and their shared history. If that's broken apart for parts, like scrap metal, that's when everything else starts to crumble, too."

Ryan pressed a kiss to her forehead and began to stack the books neatly on her bedside table, pausing to look at one she'd already opened. It showed a full colour image of Cuthbert's cross, down to the finest, tarnished detail.

"I wonder how it was cracked," he murmured, referring to the hairline fissure that ran along one side.

"People say it was cracked and repaired while Cuthbert was alive, and that the underside of the cross was worn down because that's where he used to hold it when he prayed. Maybe he felt it was too perfect, otherwise."

Ryan set the book down and smiled at the woman he loved.

"You're perfect to me."

"Even with my shaved head and all these bumps and bruises?" she said, trying to laugh about it.

"You've never been more beautiful to me than you are right now."

He moved around the bed to lie beside her until she slept— and this time, it was a long and dreamless rest.

* * *

Ryan lay awake for a while longer, wondering why it was that, despite having recovered one of the nation's most prized artefacts, he felt so little satisfaction.

It was true that one of the men responsible for hurting his wife and for stealing the cross still might not be brought to justice through the courts. There were some who would say he'd face a higher justice, but Ryan preferred to believe in more tangible examples, in the here and now.

Then there was the problem of Edward Faber. What part had he played in all this, and what transgression had he made, to warrant such a vicious death?

And he still was yet to find the person who killed Joan Tebbutt.

These unanswered questions kept him awake until the early hours, when finally he fell into an exhausted sleep.

Ryan never heard his mother's quiet tread along the landing, or the twist of the door handle as she came to check he was all right. She watched them both for a moment, then shut the door quietly once more.

Only then could Eve sleep too.

* * *

It came to Ryan shortly before dawn.

He sat bolt upright and then, careful not to wake his wife, skirted around the bed to find the book he'd been looking at the previous evening, the one which had a close-up image of Cuthbert's cross as its centrefold.

Wishing he was wrong, but fearing he would be right, Ryan flipped open the page.

There it was again, he thought. The long, hairline crack, where the cross had been broken at some earlier time.

Except, the cross he'd held in his hand the previous evening, which he'd recovered from the fuel cap of a dead man's car, had boasted a shorter crack—he was sure of it.

A tiny detail, he thought. Maybe it was nothing.

Maybe it was his fevered, sleep-starved brain playing tricks on him.

On the other hand, maybe he was right.

They'd know, soon enough.

CHAPTER 28

Thursday, 19ᵗʰ March

The mood at Northumbria Police Headquarters could only be described as jubilant.

Phillips greeted him with a cheery wave, and then pointed at a tray of pastries and fruit, sent down by Chief Constable Morrison as a small token of thanks. Ryan looked at it, and them, and didn't have the heart to voice his private concerns about the cross they'd found the night before; he was no expert, after all, and he might yet be wrong.

"Briefing in ten minutes," he told them, and went off in search of coffee.

Phillips caught up with him in the queue for the Pie Van, which had diversified to become a purveyor of fine coffee in brown cardboard cups, its owner having taken to wearing a glossy beard and a tweed waistcoat to complete the look.

"Ten americanos, please," Ryan said.

"You look as if you need all of them, today," Phillips quipped. "Bad night?"

"You could say that," Ryan muttered, and fished out a crisp twenty from his wallet.

"Howay, you can tell Uncle Frank," Phillips said, taking the tray of coffee from the server with a smile of thanks. "I know we've still got a few unanswered questions, but it's good news about the cross, at least. I thought you'd be made up about it."

"I was," Ryan said. "I am."

"You've got a face like a slapped arse," Phillips said, roundly. "Are you disappointed we couldn't bring the bloke in and sweat him a bit? I know I am."

That brought a weak smile to Ryan's face, and he reached for one of the coffees in the tray, knocking back a healthy gulp before answering.

"Yes, I'm disappointed he won't feel the weight of my boot up his arse," Ryan admitted. "But, it's not that, Frank. I have a feeling about that cross…I keep asking myself, why was Faber involved in any of this? Why did he contact Tebbutt?"

"Faber was one of those weasels who had his fingers in all kinds of pies," Phillips said. "He could have been involved in any number of ways; we just haven't worked that part out yet. There's still time to trace the other robber, and find out who wanted the cross in the first place. It'll all come together—you'll see."

Ryan wanted to believe him.

"Besides, it's put Morrison in a fine fettle," Phillips continued. "She's even talking about springing for an 'away day' for the lot of us."

"That's all we need," Ryan said. "A long weekend at some old army barracks, so we can bond over climbing walls and canoeing."

Phillips laughed.

"Aye, we get plenty of that in the day job. I'll tell her that a slap-up meal down at the *New Delhi* will do us just fine."

* * *

The celebratory atmosphere continued into Conference Room B, where there was almost a full house, word having no doubt spread that there were free pastries to be had.

Ryan's sense of foreboding did not pass, and he approached the front of the room with the air of a man expecting to receive bad news at any moment.

"Ah, thank you all for turning out this morning," he said.

He reached for his mobile phone and was about to set it to 'silent' mode, as he normally would ahead of a briefing with his team, but decided to keep the ringer on, this time.

"I'm sure you're all aware of the developments last night, and that we were able to recover a cross from the farmhouse, where one of the men responsible for the robbery was found dead."

Ryan hitched a hip onto the side of the desk, and placed his phone on the top, within easy reach.

"Prior to that, we established a connection between a man called Edward Faber—street name, Faberge—and the robbery, as well as a connection with the late DCI Joan Tebbutt. For that reason, we'll be treating the two investigations as linked, with myself and DCI MacKenzie continuing to lead on each strand, whilst managing the overall strategy together."

MacKenzie nodded her agreement.

"As regards the robbery, our working theory is that these two robbers—both of whose movements were captured on the cathedral's CCTV footage—were in league with Faberge. Unbeknownst to them, Faberge, possibly owing to his longstanding relationship with Durham Constabulary, decided at the last minute to turn them in. He rang DCI Tebbutt last Sunday night, and they spoke for around forty minutes. Tebbutt began her career working in the Fraud Team before more recently moving into Major Crimes, so it's a safe bet that she and Faberge were already well acquainted, and indeed, his number is detailed in a private address book she kept of the informants and other useful contacts she knew. Somehow, the robbers got wind of this development and killed Edward Faber either on the same night, or the following day—when they also killed Joan Tebbutt, to prevent her from investigating further or interfering with their plans."

Ryan paused, wondering whether now was the time to set out his own, alternative theory about what happened, but decided to wait until the results of the authentication came back.

"After the robbery, the two men made a safe getaway in a Citroen Picasso—"

"Glamorous," Lowerson quipped, and there were a few laughs around the room.

"—which they dumped at the side of the A1, around fifteen minutes later, and transferred into what we now believe to have been two separate vehicles. The robbers travelled to the same place, which, thanks to DC Yates' outstanding work yesterday, we now know to have been Windy Side Farm, near Hamsterley Forest."

Ryan glanced down at his mobile phone, then up at the clock on the wall.

"We, ah, believe there was an argument, resulting in one robber killing the other at point blank range. The remaining robber tried to find the cross, which had been hidden by the deceased for safekeeping, without success. Fearing discovery, the surviving robber was forced to abandon their search and escape in their own vehicle, which has yet to be traced."

Morrison chose that moment to step into the conference room, looking supremely pleased.

"Forgive the interruption, but I wanted to stop in to thank you all for your remarkable efforts in recovering the cross," she said. "And, DC Yates? I've received four separate recommendations that your work, in particular, is to be commended, and I want to let you know I'm in full agreement. You're all a credit to this constabulary, and to the force."

It was true, Ryan thought, and was also the reason he didn't have the heart to burst their bubble.

Not just yet.

"Thank you, ma'am," he said, instead.

"Well, I don't want to keep you. Ryan, MacKenzie, if there's anything you need in the way of resources, you know where to find me. Keep up the good work, everyone."

Yates looked fit to burst with pride, Ryan thought, and was happy to see it. Melanie Yates was a dedicated, hardworking woman with an eye for detail and a stomach made of iron; in a job like theirs, she had the recipe for success, and he saw no reason why she couldn't go all the way to the top, one day.

If she wanted to, of course.

"Turning to the murder of DCI Tebbutt—"

His mobile phone began to ring, interrupting his train of thought. Looking down, he saw that the caller was Tom Faulkner.

"Excuse me, everyone, I'm afraid I need to answer this," he said, and appealed to MacKenzie to take over the briefing while he stepped outside.

"Tom, what have you got for me?"

At the other end of the line, Faulkner barely knew where to start.

"It's bad news, Ryan."

He knew it.

"Tell me."

"I—I can hardly believe I'm saying this, but—"

"The cross is a replica?"

"How did you know?" Faulkner asked, in a shocked tone. "I've only just had the news from Doctor Ahern, over at the university."

Ryan didn't bother to go into it.

"What did she find?"

"She tested the metal, first thing this morning," Faulkner said. "The results are conclusive; there's absolutely no way that cross can be more than thirty years old. The same applies to the garnets. She tested those, too, and they're copies—just semi-precious gemstones. Then, there's the crack on the underside—"

"It wouldn't be too short, would it?"

Faulkner was stumped again.

"Have you been speaking to her?"

"No, just reading my wife's textbooks," Ryan replied.

"Well, you're absolutely right," Faulkner said. "The crack is four millimetres shorter than the original."

"So, it's a fake," Ryan confirmed. "The question is, what's happened to the real one?"

Faulkner sighed.

"I'm sorry to be the bearer of bad news," he said. "I wish—"

But Ryan was struck with an idea.

"Tom, get in touch with Doctor Ahern and ask her if she'd agree to sign a non-disclosure agreement, or give us her solemn word as to keeping this confidential. That goes for you, too. Have you told anybody else about this?"

"Me? No, not yet—"

"Then, don't," Ryan said firmly. "This thing is much bigger than any of us thought, and it may help us to play the fools for a while longer. Can you get on board with that?"

"If it helps to recover the real thing, count me in."

* * *

Ryan stepped back into the room and surveyed the staff who were presently seated, listening with apparent interest to what MacKenzie had to tell them. He studied each of their faces, watching every flicker, every sigh, and wondered who among them could be trusted.

"Something's come up," he said, injecting a bit of levity into his voice, so as not to cause alarm. "I'm afraid we'll have to pick up the briefing later."

Ryan stood by the door, smiling at the staff who filed out, pastries in hand.

And, when Phillips would have joined them, he put a hand on his arm and spoke in an undertone.

"Frank, round up the other three—we've got a situation."

Phillips' face betrayed nothing of what had just been said, and he popped a half-eaten pain au chocolat between his teeth before ambling over to have a quiet word in the ears of the other three members of their close-knit team.

But after the others had left, he became serious once more.

"What is it? Is it Anna?"

Ryan shook his head.

"No, I'm pleased to say she's getting better every day," he said. "This concerns the cross we recovered last night."

"Don't tell me it's been lifted again?" Phillips cried.

"It's a fake."

Phillips' mouth formed a comical 'o' of surprise.

"Are you *sure*?"

"I've just had it from Faulkner, who had it from Dr Ahern, at the university. There's no doubt."

"But—how?"

"There are two options, here," Ryan said, moving to stand by the window, further away from prying ears at the door. "The first is that the robbers stole the real cross, which is still missing, and had this fake cross made up. But why? If they had gone to all that trouble, they would have surely used the fake cross as a substitute when they lifted the real thing."

MacKenzie nodded, following his line of thought.

"They wouldn't have needed to smash into the display case, either. If you're planning to make a quiet substitution, the idea is for nobody to find out about it. It would be a completely different kind of robbery, and more likely an inside job."

"Exactly," Ryan said. "Which brings me on to the second option, which opens up a whole new can of worms. What if—just *what if*—these robbers stole a cross which was already a fake? That would put a completely different complexion on matters."

"It changes everything," Lowerson said. "We thought Faber's repeat visits were a sign that he'd been casing the joint, ahead of a planned robbery. But we forgot where his interest lies. He's a professional forger, and was for years. He's also Durham, born and bred, with a love of local history. You could see that from the books on his shelves and the pictures on the walls of his house."

Ryan nodded.

"Sometimes, the simplest answer is the right one," he said. "What if, for the sake of argument, Faber went along to the cathedral to look at the exhibitions for the first time in a while. While he's there, he notices something unusual in the cut of the cross, its composition, or the length of the crack. He isn't your ordinary visitor, let's not forget. All the same, he doesn't believe his own eyes, at first, and he goes home to think it over. Maybe he does some research and goes back the next day, and the day after that, to study the cross before he does anything rash. Problem is, somebody sees him going back and forth, showing too much interest. Maybe they recognise him too, so they keep an eye on him. Maybe Faber starts asking around, he gets in touch with some old friends to get the word on the street, to see who might have done it. Unfortunately for him, word gets back to the person responsible, and the decision is taken to silence him—but not before he's spoken to his old friend, Joan, from CID."

Ryan glanced out of the window at the city skyline, then back at his friends.

"He was trying to do the right thing, by calling Joan," he said. "But by bringing her into it, he signed her death warrant. They must have tortured him until he revealed that he had told her of his suspicions, then ransacked his house to make sure he hadn't left any notes."

"Why would they go to such extreme lengths?" Yates wondered aloud. "Why go to all that trouble?"

"To conceal the original theft, which was much more important," Ryan answered. "The real cross might have been stolen a month ago, six months ago, or several years ago; we have no way of knowing, yet. But, if I were planning to make a quiet switch, I'd think about doing it at a time when there was already going to be some upheaval."

"The renovation works," MacKenzie said. "They refitted the Great Kitchen a couple of years ago, and installed brand new display cases, along with the new security system. It would've made sense to do it then."

They were silent for a moment, and the sounds of city traffic filtered through the window from the road below.

"What do you want to do?" Phillips asked. "If you're right about this, we need to go back to square one and look at everything again."

"More than that, Frank. We need to look at who had access over the past three years, and how the switch could have been made. There's something else we haven't managed to answer, which is *why* they're going to so much trouble—not just to switch the cross in the first place but to plan and execute the subsequent robbery. Why were they willing to do all that—and to kill Faber and Tebbutt—just to make sure nobody discovered the substitution?"

"If it was an inside job, they could've been worried that the trail would lead straight to them if it became known that the cross was a fake—so worried that they staged the robbery to cast suspicion elsewhere," MacKenzie suggested.

Ryan's eyes narrowed. "I hope you're right about that, Denise—because if you are, they must have some reason to fear that we can trace them. However, you look at it, they've gone to a lot of trouble to steal this cross twice."

"It's obviously special to them," Yates said.

"I'm beginning to wonder about the other artefacts," Ryan said. "Is the cross itself special to them, or all of Cuthbert's relics? If it's the latter, there was nothing to stop a person of sufficient means switching several of the artefacts, and creating quite a collection for themselves."

"This is enormous," Lowerson muttered. "People are going to go crazy, when they find out."

"They're not going to find out. At least, not just yet," Ryan said. "I've asked Faulkner and Ahern to keep this to themselves for a while longer, in the strictest of confidence, and I'm going to ask the same of you. If I'm right about all this, we're not just looking for some rich collector—we're looking for a ruthless mastermind. We won't be able to conduct any kind of investigation if this goes public, because it'll drive them underground. No," he said. "I want whoever is behind this to believe their dummy robbery has been a success, and that we're congratulating ourselves at having restored the real thing to its rightful resting place. They want us to believe we have the real cross, so let's play the fools for a while longer, and see what we uncover."

He looked to each of them in turn, and received a firm nod.

"What about Morrison?"

"I'll speak to her," Ryan said. "She's no blabbermouth. But, aside from that, this needs to remain strictly within our circle."

"What about Tebbutt?" Phillips asked.

"I've got an update on that," Yates told them. "When we used the robber's mobile phone number to pinpoint the location of Windy Side Farm yesterday, we assumed the number belonged to the robber who turned up dead—"

"Do we have an ID on him, by the way?" Ryan interrupted.

"Not yet," she replied. "We're running it through the DNA database, right now."

Ryan nodded, and gestured for her to continue.

"We assumed the mobile number belonged to his burner mobile, but what if it belonged to the other robber? Sir, I had a word with the phone company this morning and they say the number is no longer active, which means they're probably aware that we raided the farmhouse last night—"

"Has that been made public, yet?" Ryan asked.

"Not to my knowledge, sir."

The light of battle began to shine in his eyes.

"I see. They disposed of the burner mobile, or at least removed the SIM card, so we're unable to trace its current whereabouts."

"Yes—but we can trace its *previous* whereabouts," Yates said.

"You're a crafty one!" Phillips told her.

She grinned.

"Anyway, I went back to the phone company and asked them to send me a list of the times and dates that mobile number had checked in to the various masts in the area, and I've uncovered something interesting."

She made a grab for her file and hurriedly plucked out a printed spreadsheet which she'd already taken the trouble to highlight.

"If you look here, at the yellow columns, you'll see there's a pattern. This mobile number checked in to the same mast, without fail, every Monday for the past six weeks, which is as far back as the data runs."

"Do we know where the mast is?" Ryan asked.

Yates nodded, and told him the address. If Ryan was surprised, nothing of it showed on his face, which remained hard and resolute.

He turned to Phillips.

"Grab your coat, Frank. We've got an arrest to make."

CHAPTER 29

For the second time that week, Ryan and Phillips paid a visit to their neighbouring constabulary. This time, there was none of the awkwardness or nerves there had been the first time around. Righteous anger had taken their place, and the sure-fire knowledge that Joan Tebbutt would have done exactly the same thing without hesitation.

"Where's Carter?" Ryan asked the desk sergeant, who took one look at his face and hurriedly buzzed them through the security door.

"I think I saw him heading down to the changing rooms," she said. "In the basement, one floor down."

They took the stairs rather than waiting for the lifts, and emerged into a wide corridor which led to a small gym and changing room area in one direction, and the custody suite in the other.

They found the young man on the rowing machine.

"Carter."

He looked up from his programmed workout, and then hit the 'END' button.

"This is a surprise," he said. "Sorry, I didn't know you were coming, or I'd have made sure I was ready to meet you," he said.

"Never mind that," Ryan said. "Where's Winter?"

Carter was surprised.

"I know she hasn't given you a statement, yet, and I'm sorry about that—"

"I asked you where she was," Ryan snapped.

"She's at home, I expect—Justine had to take her brother to another appointment at the hospital this morning, so she needed to take the day off."

"What's wrong with her brother?" Phillips asked.

"He has a degenerative disease," Carter said. "He also suffers from severe learning disabilities. Justine has to take him to a regular appointment at the hospital on Mondays, but sometimes other things crop up. Unfortunately, Justine's father has never been in the picture, and her mum passed away from breast cancer a couple of years ago. We try to be accommodating. What's this all about?"

But before Ryan could answer, Carter's mobile phone began to ring.

"Sorry," he muttered. "It's the front desk."

"Yes?"

His face registered a range of emotions, from surprise, to confusion and, finally, sadness.

"Right, thanks. I'll take care of it."

Carter ended the call, and looked between the two men.

"That was Durham University Hospital," he said. "They say Justine left Danny at the hospital this morning, and she hasn't come back to fetch him. What's going on here?"

"We'll tell you on the way," Ryan replied. "Hurry up."

* * *

The journey to Justine Winter's home in the small village of Aykley Heads took less than fifteen minutes, during which time Ryan and Phillips acquainted Carter with several pertinent facts he had not known about his constable. At first, he was unwilling to accept the possibility of them being true and Ryan had to admire the man's loyalty to his staff, as well as his tenacity in questioning their facts. It was a foolish man who took the world for granted and, as they'd already come to understand, Ben Carter was far from being a foolish man. When presented with the telephone data, showing the robber's burner mobile having been present for six weeks at the hospital every Monday, and tallying with Justine's regular appointment to attend with her brother, the coincidence was too great to be believed.

"At least give her a chance to explain. There must be some explanation for all this," Carter said, mostly to himself.

"We aren't in the business of haranguing people, but we're talking about a woman who facilitated the murder of your friend and DCI," Ryan snapped. "We'll do whatever has to be done to ascertain the truth."

Carter nodded, thinking of the woman he'd come to know, and trying to understand how he could have been so blind.

"The CCTV footage at the cathedral showed two men," he muttered. "I thought they were both men?"

Ryan shook his head.

"One is clearly male, the other was of average height and build, and wore a jacket and a backpack. Neither of them ever looked directly at the cameras, so we only ever had partial imagery. Justine wears her hair in a short style. It's easy to mistake the gender in those circumstances."

As they turned into Justine's road, Carter spotted her car parked further down the street.

"She's home," he said. "That's her car."

"Right, now, here's what I want you to do," Ryan said, parking the car a few doors away. "I want you to go and knock on the door first, to put her at her ease. We'll follow in a few minutes. She knows we discovered the farmhouse, which means she may also know we'll have been tracing her burner mobile, even though she's now stopped using it. It was a mistake to keep it on her person; she should have done what it says on the tin and burned it after the first use."

Carter nodded, and slammed out of the car.

They watched him walk along the pavement, his shoulders slumped, and then straighten himself up as he approached her front door.

"He's got more mettle than I gave him credit for," Phillips remarked.

But something else had occurred to Ryan.

"Frank, why would she leave her brother at the hospital?"

"What's that?"

"The hospital rang to say she'd left her brother there, and not come back to collect him. Why would she do that, unless—"

They looked at one another and then swore volubly.

"She doesn't plan to go back, so she needed to put him in a safe place," Ryan muttered. "Shit."

They ran towards the front door, where Carter was still knocking loudly and calling her name.

"She's not answering," he said.

"Stand aside, son," Phillips told him.

He gave the door a couple of hard kicks and then the wood splintered and swung open to reveal an empty hallway beyond.

"Justine?" Carter called out. "Justine!"

CHAPTER 30

One week later

Winter had chosen to do it in her bedroom, using the same handgun she'd used to kill Joan Tebbutt. She'd muffled the sound using one of her pillows, which explained the confetti of duck feathers sticking to the coagulating blood which formed a halo around her head.

She'd tried her best not to cause any damage to the property, since it was a rental, and had taken the trouble to cover the floor with plastic sheeting, so as to protect the carpet. She even left an envelope with some cash to cover the cost of a new mattress and any redecorating that might be necessary following her death.

They found nothing whatsoever that would provide any insight or clue as to how she'd become involved in the cathedral robbery, but Justine had still chosen to leave them a message, to do with as they wished. She'd chosen to have three items resting beside her on the bed when she died. First, there was a framed picture of her and her brother, on the back of which she'd written, "I'm sorry, Danny, I did my best. I love you." Second, a photocopy of the life insurance policy she had taken out some time ago, detailing that the policy would still pay out even if the insured takes their own life—the sum would cover the costs of her brother's ongoing care. Third, a single sheet of paper, upon which she'd written a cryptic, one-word note, which they were presently unable to read as it consisted of symbols rather than letters.

"I wish I knew what the hell this is supposed to mean," Ryan said, one sunny afternoon the following week. "I'll have to bring in a symbologist, or whatever they call themselves."

"It's written in runes," Anna told him, barely glancing up from the book she was reading. "Those symbols are part of the runic alphabets, which people used to use in the old Germanic languages, before the Latin alphabet was adopted more widely. If you want to find out more, I've got several books on the history of runes in my study."

"How the heck do you know all this?"

"Common knowledge," she said.

"What does this one word say?"

Anna glanced across at the paper in his hand, trying to remember the meaning of the different symbols.

"I think that word says, 'SACRIFICE'," she said, quietly. "Would that make sense to you?"

Ryan frowned, thinking of Justine Winter's motivations. Even to the last, she'd thought of her brother, and not herself.

"Yes, I think it might," he replied, and thought of the woman he'd known only briefly. Winter had been a logical woman, well thought of by her peers, all of whom had expressed complete shock at the news of her deception. Time and again, he'd heard the same phrase repeated from different mouths: "it just wasn't like her."

Had her actions been out of character? Ryan wondered. There were people in the world who kept their true selves well hidden, sociopathic types who could adapt their nature to suit an audience. Had Justine Winter fallen into that category?

His gut told him that the answer was *no*.

She'd be reviled and hated as a cop-killer and a traitor throughout the corridors of Durham Constabulary and beyond. There was nothing Ryan could do about that, nor anything he would particularly wish to do, for Justine Winter had taken two lives, and almost contributed to the loss of the lives of his wife and child. There was insufficient evidence to say, conclusively, whether Winter had also played a part in the death of Edward Faber, but the manner and style was entirely different from her preferred method—which was, of course, a quick gunshot to the head. That kind of killer took no pleasure from the act; they sought to get it over with as quickly and painlessly as possible, much as they would wish to relieve a dying animal from its pain.

Given his suspicions about there being some unseen, controlling hand behind the false robbery and perhaps other incidents they had yet to uncover, Ryan was forced to consider the possibility that Winter had been acting under duress. Organised criminals, of every variety, were constantly on the lookout for individuals in positions of authority, who are also prone to bribery or coercion, to further their own ends. In Justine Winter's case, her brother had been her Achilles' heel, and there was nothing she wouldn't do to ensure his happiness; even on the day of her own suicide.

Had some unscrupulous person singled her out?

"I was thinking about the Cuthbert connection," Anna said, suddenly.

Ryan turned to her.

"What about it?"

"You already know that some people believed—and probably still believe—that he could perform miracles. The same applies to his relics, after he died. People are convinced they have healing properties."

"What are you thinking?" he asked. "You think somebody's taken the cross because they're unwell?"

"Maybe. It's a possibility, isn't it? What if they want the cross because they think it has healing properties?"

Ryan closed his eyes, thinking of the far-reaching possibilities if that was the case.

And he thought again of Justine Winter's brother, whose disease was degenerative, and would ultimately kill him.

Had she believed that her actions would lead to some sort of cure? Had somebody used her vulnerability to convince her to do these unspeakable things, in some kind of twisted quid pro quo?

If she'd made a deal with the devil, had Justine left her message of sacrifice for the police, or for somebody else, entirely?

Ryan looked across to where his wife was sitting up in bed, sipping from a tall glass of water. There was something, or *someone*, evil lurking beneath all that had happened over the past week. He'd thought it would be a case of finding the bad guys, and locking them away, just as usual. He hadn't considered there might be a deeper layer, something infinitely more terrifying to contemplate.

Because, if they'd managed to get away with it, unseen and unnoticed until now, who could say how many people had been hurt, or compromised, or used as proxies for another's bidding?

"Is everything alright?" Anna asked.

Ryan pasted a smile on his face, unwilling to allow anything to make her anxious at such a critical time in her recovery, and so close to their baby girl's arrival. There was nothing he wouldn't do to protect the ones he loved, but now he feared he'd brought a new threat into their lives.

"Everything's fine," he said. "Can I get you anything?"

Anna shook her head, and went back to her reading, while Ryan headed downstairs and did something he hadn't done in a long while.

He asked for help.

"Dad?"

Charles Ryan looked up from his daily inspection of the newspaper, and set it aside as he saw the ashen look on his son's face.

"What is it?"

"I'm going to need your help. I've stumbled into something dangerous, and I'm worried about Anna and the baby."

Charles removed his glasses and folded them neatly.

"We'll be there to support you, whatever the future holds," he said. "Never fear, son."

Eve watched her husband and son exchange a hard embrace, and put a hand to her heart, thanking whichever moon or star had granted her deepest wish.

They were a family again.

* * *

The shrine was hidden deep underground, and was accessible via a single door to which only they had the key. It was a private sanctum, not a thoroughfare for the hoi polloi; a place where they could regenerate, and be reborn each morning.

It was a trove of family heirlooms, each painstakingly recovered from their place of captivity, no longer to be gawped at by an ignorant rabble. Their treasures shone in the candlelight, not beneath the garish light of an electric bulb. This was a world of reverence and contemplation, of power and the powerful.

It was a place unlike any other, because it was intended for no other.

It had taken years to build, and still more to maintain—such was the cycle of their immortality. To have the blood was not enough; they must also be imbued with the power, and the knowledge of what it could bring.

Cuthbert's ancestor knew what it meant to remain humble.

It did no good to fly too close to the sun, like poor Icarus; they must remain worthy of all that they had been granted.

Sometimes, a sacrifice was needed.

They crawled inside the cell, an exact replica of the one Cuthbert had built on Inner Farne, and pressed a concealed button. Immediately, sounds of deafening waves and rushing wind mingled with birds of prey, and they closed their eyes, waiting for the voice to speak again.

EPILOGUE

Elsie Kaye spent a lot of her time watching people. They came to visit their family and friends, or they bustled around the hospital tending the sick, and many of them stopped to say 'hello' to the foolish old woman with lilac hair.

She knew that's what they must think of her.

Old and foolish.

What could a woman of her years know about life, and love, after all?

Only that which could be learned from eighty years of living.

She saw their impatience and their awkwardness when she talked for too long. The young didn't always want to be reminded of the old, though she might have said the feeling was mutual.

While they looked upon her faded skin and bony hands and dreaded what was to come, she looked upon their smooth bodies and strong muscles and was reminded of all that she'd lost.

She still remembered, you see.

Each night, when she slept, she remembered life as it used to be, and each morning when she wakened, she realised that was no longer how it was.

She wasn't a girl in platform shoes and a polkadot miniskirt, dancing to The Beatles or The Rolling Stones.

Now, the dancing was done mostly in her head.

She wasn't a newlywed bride, learning how to be a woman with the man she'd loved. The man with the auburn hair and green eyes had left this world, never to return, and all she had left were the memories, and children who hadn't yet learned that life was fleeting.

A little boy stuck his tongue out as he left the ward, and she stuck hers out too, to make him giggle.

When all else failed, it was best to laugh.

The ward was quiet again, the visitors gone and the old fogies all asleep, after their exertions.

She cast around for an occupation, but she'd read all of her books and had never learned how to knit.

"These came for you, Mrs Kaye!"

Elsie turned to see a young nurse walking towards her, carrying an enormous bouquet of red roses. Not just any roses, either; the big, velvety Grand Prix roses, with the blood-red petals.

"I think you must have made a mistake, love—these can't be for me."

Nobody would send these for her.

"They're definitely for you," the nurse told her. "Shall I read out the card?"

Elsie ran her fingertips over the soft petals and nodded dumbly.

"It says, 'For Mrs Kaye, the most glamorous girl on Ward 18. With love from, a Secret Admirer.'"

Elsie smiled, and felt much more like her old self.

"They're from my toyboy," she said, with a wink.

ABOUT THE AUTHOR

LJ Ross is an international bestselling author, best known for creating atmospheric mystery and thriller novels, including the DCI Ryan series of Northumbrian murder mysteries which have sold over four million copies worldwide.

Her debut, *Holy Island*, was released in January 2015 and reached number one in the UK and Australian charts. Since then, she has released a further nineteen novels, all of which have been top three global bestsellers and fifteen of which have been UK #1 bestsellers. Louise has garnered an army of loyal readers through her storytelling and, thanks to them, several of her books reached the coveted #1 spot whilst only available to pre-order ahead of release.

Louise was born in Northumberland, England. She studied undergraduate and postgraduate Law at King's College, University of London and then abroad in Paris and Florence. She spent much of her working life in London, where she was a lawyer for a number of years until taking the decision to change career and pursue her dream to write. Now, she writes full time and lives with her husband and son in Northumberland. She enjoys reading all manner of books, travelling and spending time with family and friends.

If you enjoyed *The Shrine*, please consider leaving a review online.

If you would like to be kept up to date with new releases from LJ Ross, please complete an e-mail contact form on her Facebook page or website, www.ljrossauthor.com

Printed in Great Britain
by Amazon